Sweet Child of Mine

Holly Winter

Thank you to those who encouraged me to write this book - you know who you are. This book is dedicated to you.

The truth was always inside of me - never outside. Metin Hara says, "The mind directs you to the illusion and the heart to the truth. Whichever you listen to, you will find yourself there". Once I started listening to my heart, I set myself free. Until you become who you are supposed to be, you will live in illusion. Now that I've written this book, I can finally leave the past behind and bury the dead. Life is just beginning, and the heart's pathway awaits.

I hope you follow your heart, if not already. It could save your life.

Discretion Advised

This novel contains themes and discussions of child abuse that may be disturbing or triggering for some readers. Reader discretion is advised.

If you would like to read the prequel, *Under Her Watchful Eye,* and find out what happened to Ava right before the events of this book, get the free novella at:

https://BookHip.com/WCPBRKC

Contents

Chapter 1

Ava took another sip of champagne from the glass. The drink felt good as it slid down her throat, and she knew that she suspected that she might not deserve the celebration. Every last drop tasted good. Perhaps someday, she would feel she had worked to sell a home in London.

Kate moved quickly, passed by her, carrying three sparkling flutes. "Drink up," she said. "You deserve this."

Kate was the woman closest to her age, thirty-five, at the real estate company. She had dark hair that came down to her shoulders. However, Kate was not an agent; she served more as a woman of all trades in the office. Ava had worked in that position before Kate. The job suited her, was not too taxing, and she rarely had to put herself out to be scrutinised by the bosses. She could provide schedules for everyone in the office and knew the status of every listing there.

Ava laughed. "It certainly looks like you're having a few."

Kate shrugged, making the glasses on the tray shake. "They're not mine." Six flutes were lined up on the tray, and Ava wondered how many of the glasses were empty now.

The celebration was held at the corporate headquarters of Jones & Jenkins Real Estates in London. The glass windows ran the length of the wall, giving the partiers a view like few others. The sun had gone down now, and the lights of the buildings shone into the reception space.

Kate nodded toward the men standing in the distance –the bosses of the real estate company. Of course, even during a celebration, they would expect to be served.

Ava finished her glass and decided to go talk to the men. She wanted to ensure they knew about her tremendous sales, even if it had fallen into her lap.

Malcolm greeted her first. "Ava, you look radiant. Congratulations on the house in Ealing." He made a face as if middle-class housing was not for him. Ava knew better; there wasn't any such thing as cheap housing in London. There wasn't anything affordable in London.

She smiled and held up her glass. Only a tiny sip was left in the glass. Malcolm took it as a request for more and asked Kate to fetch more glasses. That had not been Ava's intention.

Malcolm smiled again and moved closer to her. He was always a bit of a flirt, even when he was slightly insulting her sales. Her trim figure, blonde hair, and green eyes had made her an interest to many company men. Ava had to walk that tight line between keeping her job and being nice to the boss.

She had to admit that Malcolm was attractive. With his slicked-back dark hair and intense blue eyes, Ava found herself interested in the man. He was tall and always immaculately dressed. He clearly worked out with his lithe frame, but Ava had no idea when that would be. He worked twelve hours a day at the office, if not more. Malcolm supposedly had a girlfriend, but Ava had never met this woman in her years here. The gossip in the office was that he invented a fake date to keep the agents in the office away and the clients looking to fill a family home with him.

The other two men were older and had no interest in a thirty-five-year-old. According to them, she was over the hill. They preferred the younger girls, and Ava felt old for a second, even though she was far from retirement. Chris had a woman on his arm who couldn't have been older than twenty. Gary's date looked like she was challenging the other to see who the youngest plus-one in attendance was. The girls seemed to be competing about which could show the most flesh that evening. Gary's date was winning—if Ava had been the judge.

Kate brought back another glass of champagne. "Cheers to Ava," she said, without a smile now. Perhaps she wanted to be toasted by the others and not simply the person in charge of bringing drinks.

The guests all raised their glasses and drank again. Ava blushed a little, feeling her face burn. It had been a long time since she'd made a sale. She'd been concerned that the bosses would ask her to leave for the last two months. She didn't feel that she added enough to the business.

At least for the moment, she had lost that fear. The bosses had seen her in action and would keep her around—for now.

She glanced at her watch. Simon had yet to arrive. They had not been dating long, but he had never been known for being punctual. He came and went as he pleased. She pursed her lips and excused herself. She would call him and see where he was at.

Even though they'd only been going out a few months, Ava had felt an immediate connection to the man. He was thin with red-blond hair and glasses that made him look like he could read her mind to see what she was thinking. It was too early to think of anything more than dating him. However, Ava had considered where they would live and what they would do in their spare time.

She'd met his family twice, and they'd all seemed to like her. On the other hand, Ava had explicitly made it clear that Simon would not be meeting her family. She did not want to go to York to see them; fortunately, they would not visit London. The mere thought of meeting her family made her stomach roil.

Pulling out her phone, she noticed several phone calls and voicemails. She didn't recognise the number. "I'll deal with them tomorrow," she said to herself. She put a hand over her mouth. She might have had too much to drink if she'd begun talking to herself. She would need to make sure that this was the last drink.

She took a deep breath and let the air out. Ava pressed the buttons she knew so well and waited for Simon to answer. However, instead, the call went straight to voicemail. She looked at the phone, shocked that he hadn't answered. Where had he gone?

It was unlike Simon's not calling or letting her know what was happening, and Ava worried for a second. Had he decided that she was not good enough for him? She'd had that happen before. A good start, followed by the man ghosting her with no explanation of what had gone wrong. The champagne was getting to her, and she didn't care to have her mood destroyed by the situation.

She returned to the other room, where her coworkers were still drinking and laughing. Happy to stand back away from the crowd, Ava had a moment or two where she didn't have to participate. To be honest, she felt like something of a fraud here. Yes, she had sold the property. Yes, the market is terrible. However, she managed to sell the property through luck rather than ability.

The buyer had not been hers. She had not scrambled across leads and contacts to find the buyer. It had all happened quickly. She had been waiting for a client to walk through the house, counting the moments until she could leave without appearing impatient. She rechecked her watch, and when she looked up, she saw a couple standing before her.

"Hello," the woman had said. "Are you an agent by any chance?"

While Ava didn't feel like an agent, she agreed that she was. The couple asked for a tour, and Ava gladly walked them around the eight flats that made up the rental property. Four of the tenants had already agreed to open their flats for the showing, and Ava had not bothered to give the renters the names of the potential buyers. So, they would never know the difference.

Ava finished the walk-through and smiled at the pair, who were grinning with every muscle on their face. She had the notion that they were going to make an offer.

And they did – the next day without any changes or corrections to the contract. It was the easiest sale she'd ever made.

Ava smiled again as she thought of the couple and their dreams for the property. She also smiled because the sale had killed the slump of the last several months. She had sold a property at the asking price in a weak market. The bosses were satisfied, and she was pleased.

She looked at her watch again. Still no sign of Simon, and it was nearly time for the party to end. A few of the coworkers had already left, needing a whole night's sleep before trying to sell another house the next day. Ava knew she'd be coming in late tomorrow, but she'd receive new listings.

Malcolm saw her and waved. "Need a ride home?" he asked.

She smiled. That invitation had led to situations with other women. She had learned from their stories. "Thanks, but I'm going downstairs now. Simon's meeting me."

"Too bad he didn't come up," Malcolm said. His eyes squinted as if he knew that she was lying.

"He just finished up with his workday and not feeling well." She smiled and waved again.

Now that Ava had lied to him, she felt compelled to leave. She went down the stairs and out into the drizzling rain. She pulled her hood over her hair and headed to the tube station.

She'd still had no message from Simon when she arrived home at her one-bedroom flat. She took the Victoria line to the Highbury and Islington station. Granted, the line was not known for its mobile reception, but she still expected a text or voicemail message.

She recalled the multiple calls she'd missed but refused to ruin tonight's celebration with more work. She'd done her duty and now wanted a break.

The flat was dark when she arrived home. For a second, she felt like someone was or had been here. Ava thought she'd caught the whiff of a man's cologne or perhaps just his presence. She called out. "Simon?" but the flat was quiet. She wondered about it and then decided to try to call Simon again.

The phone went directly to voicemail, and she decided that would be the last effort to contact him tonight. She didn't want the reputation of being a nag so early in their relationship, even though he'd skipped a big night for her.

She started getting prepared for bed. While brushing her teeth, Ava thought she heard the phone again. When she looked at the display on the iPhone, the notification was the same number as before. Now concerned that she had missed a call from Simon at a number she didn't recognise, she dialed the number and waited.

"Ava," a voice said. This was definitely not Simon. The voice was harsh and raspy, unlike Simon's melodious voice.

"Speaking," Ava replied after a few seconds. She was uncertain whether this call was legitimate or not.

"It's Luke," the man said. It took Ava a moment to determine who this was: the man expected to be recognised. Was he a client? He couldn't be a previous date or boyfriend. She would have remembered him.

Finally, it struck her. This was her brother. How many years had Ava not talked to Luke? Ten years, maybe—or longer? He still lived with the rest of the family in York. "Luke, I hadn't expected to hear from you tonight. What's going on?"

Her voice cracked a little when she spoke. She was not looking forward to interacting with her family again. Ava had a terrible feeling that something was wrong. Luke would never call, much less this late at night, unless something was terribly wrong. "Is it mum?"

She felt remorse for a moment, thinking that her mother's passing would almost be a blessing. For years, she had known that her mother was a mixture of undereducated and alcoholic. She felt sorry for the woman and tried to make excuses for her odd and often selfish behaviors. Still, Ava was certain that the booze had worn down her body by now.

"No, our grandfather has passed away."

Chapter 2

The sentence hit her in the gut. Her grandfather had not better cared for himself than her mother. He had drank to excess on a daily basis. He'd suffered several medical ailments over the past decade: kidneys, lungs, heart, and more. She was actually surprised that he'd survived this long.

He had been a big part of her childhood. Arthur Farley had been a constant companion when she was in primary school. She recalled him, slightly stooped and wearing dark glasses, picking her up—along with Luke—and taking them out for a bite to eat. They would return home too late to finish their homework before bed. Ava once complained about the punishments she'd received for not turning in her work. Yet, her mother told her to appreciate their grandfather's presence in their lives. Ava had grown to work on homework during her free moments in class.

Ava dreaded what was to come. The funeral would be difficult to handle, losing a member of the family. However, she expected the probate to be far more complex. The other family members would behave like vultures, swooping in and taking every piece of furniture and assets until nothing was left. Her mother, Donna, would battle them for each stick of chairs and sofas.

And it would be in York. A walled city as old as the Romans and a cathedral town to boot. She had no desire to go back there. While London had its history, the city had bits and pieces of this century, whereas the history in York and the way things were seeped into every nook in the town. She had found it oppressive then, and Ava was sure it had not improved in any way.

Ava wanted to call Simon for support and let him know she'd be gone for a few days, but she'd already wasted all her phone calls to him. Any more, and he'd wonder what he'd gotten into. Still, she wondered if he was out with friends—or another woman.

"When is the funeral?" she asked.

"Two days from now," Luke replied, "but you should come home now. It's a mess here, and I'm sure you could help smooth things out." His voice held a tinge of desperation that Ava recalled from their youth. The memories were not good. Luke was younger than Ava, and he'd looked to her for help. Luke was not the type to stand up for himself, and Ava had seen their mother bully him more times than she could count.

"I'll have to rearrange my schedule, but I'll see what I can do. I'll be there as fast as I can." Ava's thoughts suddenly turned to only York – and her family. She forgot the triumph of her sale, her relationship with Simon, and the future.

The first train out of London to York was at 4:55 a.m., but Ava did not want to get up that early after the night of celebrating. She found a later train, booked a seat, and went to bed.

When she caught the train, it was still far too early. She dozed on the trip to York and woke at the station, feeling groggy.

She hadn't expected anyone to pick her up at the station. That wasn't the way her family operated. Ava had been gone so long—of her own accord—that she would not expect a happy welcome home. There would be resentment and accusations of abandonment.

Ava managed to get her rental and started the drive to where Arthur had lived. She found her grandfather's home, thinking she would likely find someone there. Her mother was far more likely to host the visitation at his more elegant home than hers. The house had a certain charm. Ava was nearly sure that the property would also have a price tag on the family home shortly. The house had far more space than her mother's home. She would like to have sold it herself, but that was unlikely. Her mother would doubt that she had the ability to sell property.

Ava stood outside, staring at the house. She knew that her grandfather had been ill for years, but the level of disrepair shocked her.

The outside walls had moss growing from the ground level up. The plants had nearly made it to the second level of the house. Ava had remembered the house as bright and clean as a child. The windows needed to be cleaned as well. The dirt and dust had accumulated to the point that one could not see in the house at all. Perhaps he'd wanted it that way.

Two shutters had lost one or more screws, leaving them askew. Ava was surprised as she knew that her grandfather had owned the house outright and had more than enough savings to keep the house in pristine condition. Ava's mother had told her more than once that he was rich. However, in her absence, something had gone wrong with the house — and the man.

"Ava, why are you standing out there?" a voice called.

And that was the most likely item that had gone wrong — her mother. Before she could answer, the woman exited the house and came out into the ignored garden in front of the home.

She had not changed in the past several years, though she had put on a few stone. Her nose was still the bulbous red thing that reminded her of Rudoph. Ava was certain that her mother still drank Guinness Stout. The dark ale had been her favorite since the time she was a girl. Ava suspected that her mother had emulated her father, who had imbibed the stout frequently on their trips to a pub.

"Well, c'mon. What are you waiting for, a royal invitation?" her mother prompted, waving an arm.

Ava wasn't sure about entering the house. Her real estate training made her worry about vermin or mold from the look of the place. What would she do in those cases? The thought of spending her time scrubbing away the years of neglect made her cringe. While she'd just made a rather large commission from the sale of the multi-family rental, she didn't have the funds to spend the week in an Airbnb near their home.

"I'll be there in a moment," Ava said. "I'm just looking around."

Her mother, Donna, shouted across the street. Their own family house was just across the street and down a few houses from her grandfather's house. Ava sometimes wondered if their home's position was a familial bond or if Donna had wanted to keep track of him—and his money.

"Well, hurry up. We don't have all day." Donna was short and rather plump these days. Her hair had gone grey, but Ava noticed signs that her mother had tried to dye her hair. Yet the grey still showed through in places. Ava wasn't sure if that resulted from home hair coloring or a fashionable look for older women. Her mother's face had deep lines, and most seemed to result from years of frowning. Of course, Ava couldn't blame her mother for the scowl. Her father had just passed away.

That type of screaming made Ava wince. She'd heard that so many times while growing up that it brought back painful memories of her youth. It was funny how the noise brought back so many bad memories.

The most vivid recollection was the departure of her father, Oliver. He'd left after a fierce row where the couple had screamed at each other for hours. She had always thought her father had been right. No one could take that continued nagging for years. Oliver apologised for not being able to take Ava and her brother with him when he left. Despite her contempt for her children, Donna insisted that the children stay with her. The choice for Oliver had been life or the children. He had moved on without them.

Ava couldn't recall the last time she'd seen him, but it had been long before she left school. So, more than twenty years.

She still hadn't moved, although Donna had already retreated into the house. There would be no welcome home for her.

"Well, if it isn't Miss Ava," a voice said behind her. She spun around and gave a smile to the older woman.

"Mrs. Horridge," Ava said. "I didn't expect to see you here." Ava was shocked to see the frail woman walking towards her. Mrs. Horridge had been her English teacher all those years ago. The woman now walked with a cane, hunched over as she made her way down the street.

"It's you who left, dearie," said Mrs. Horridge. "Not me. I'm still here in the same house I always was. Is everything okay? I've heard you had a bad time in London."

"Yes, I'm a real estate agent there. Everything is going fine," Ava said. She wasn't sure why she'd shared that much.

"Is your head okay?" Mrs. Horridge asked.

Ava paused. "Yes, just fine." Wondering why she would ask that.

"Good for you. I hope you're doing well," the woman said. Then she stopped and looked down at her feet. "I'm sorry. I was so happy to see you. I didn't think that you'd be here for your grandfather's funeral. So, I'm sure you're *not* doing well if you're here..."

"I just got the news from the family last night."

"I'm sure you did," the woman said slightly sourly. "They

would do that."

"Do you know what happened?" Ava asked. "I mean to my grandfather."

"Now, dear, you know I was never one to gossip. Lots of stories are going around York. I would never dream of repeating them to the family. Besides, I'm sure you'll hear them for yourself soon—if you haven't already."

Ava opened her mouth to speak and then closed it again. The teacher's response was so odd that she didn't know how to answer. "I hope I'll see you later," Ava replied, thinking that was a noncommittal answer.

The woman nodded and went on her way. Ava watched her for a few minutes and decided to enter the family home. She had spent enough time outside on a cloudy, gloomy day.

The house was dark, as she'd expected from the windows. A faint, musty smell filled the air. She sniffled twice, trying not to inhale too much of the odor. At least one inhabitant had smoked vigorously, most likely with closed windows. Ava had attempted to sell too many houses to avoid recognising the stench.

She followed her old memories as she made her way to the kitchen. The darkness was too much for her eyes to find anything with only her memory.

"It's been a long time," a voice said in the dark.

Ava nearly jumped. Even though she had talked to him last night, she didn't immediately recognise the voice. She assumed it had to be Luke.

"I didn't see you sitting in the dark."

Luke stood up – as much as he could. Even though he was a few years younger than Ava, making him in his early thirties, he looked older in this light. Luke slumped. His thick brown hair was not styled. Perhaps Donna had cut it for him. He had two days of stubble on his face below his green eyes, one of the few traits the two shared. He was still thin, but while the build had made him look more attractive when he was younger, now he looked like he might be ill.

He was not the man she'd known when she left. The current man looked like the air had been let out of him, leaving him as a deflated balloon. What had happened to him?

Ava was relieved that the fire had gone out of Luke, sad as it was to say. His constant harangues in her last days in York had provided her with reasons to leave—and not return. He demanded that she stay, wanting her to accept her mother's harangues for them both.

"Glad you could make it," he said. "You're needed here."

Ava didn't respond. Perhaps it was the tone or the peculiar wording, but she felt a shiver up her spine as he spoke.

"Of course, I'd come. He's family."

Luke laughed. It was not an amused laugh but a sarcastic tone that made Ava remember those last days in York—the hate he spewed, the accusations that she wanted her grandfather's money, the desire for her to follow the same path as her father. She had not missed a day of York or the inhabitants of her family.

It was going to be a difficult few days.

Chapter 3

Dinner was the worst, though nothing so far about the trip was pleasant. Ava had been settled in her childhood bedroom. Besides the small space and the unmistakable appearance of the room, which had not been changed since she was a young girl, the room smelled of dust and smoke.

The boy band posters still hung on the wall, though their ripped corners looked like they'd been ripped. She wondered if her mother had just put those oversized adverts on the wall after she learned that Ava was returning home. If so, what had been here before that?

The bed was neatly made with a pink and grey duvet, pillows, and a few stuffed animals. Since Ava had left before age twenty, she doubted she'd still have animals on the bed. Her mother had likely brought them out of storage to try to set a scene of her younger days. What was the woman's purpose in doing so?

It was the type of thing she expected from her mother. She would keep the room as a faux shrine to her daughter, who had left them, and yet not take care of the room in any way.

A stack of photos was on the small desk in the room. Ava picked up the images and flipped through them. The memories came flooding back—those of her father especially, but also Luke, who looked younger and brighter. She had nearly forgotten these memories, the smiles and the good times. So much else had happened in the meantime. Ava wondered if Donna had put the images there or if she'd overlooked these pictorial memories.

She looked into the mirror, which hung just over the desk. Ava saw a competent young woman with no problems with her life or career. Her blonde hair was styled as she wanted—not by her mother's demands and cajoling. Standing a bit straighter, she saw someone who had made her own way. Part of Ava was wishing that she had just sent a bouquet to the funeral and stayed in London. She didn't belong here anymore.

Her stomach started to churn. Ava wanted it to be that she'd only had a cup of yogurt for breakfast, but she suspected it had more to do with her return to this house and her grandfather's death. He hadn't been well in the past few years, suffering from a type of dementia that left him unable to talk or function by himself—but still alive to read and watch the telly.

Ava had tried to visit a few times, but the comparison of the younger, more vital man and the later version of him had depressed her. Ava wasn't sure if the man recognised her as an adult. She struggled with her emotions while she visited, and she tried to remember the more familiar side of her grandfather.

She tried to remember the last time she'd seen her grandfather, but it had been years since she had been to York.

Ava grabbed the bag on her bed and pulled out a few clothes to hang in the closet. She opened the doors to the closet and gasped. Some of her adolescent garments were still in the closet. The fashions were of another age, and she tried to remember the various skirts, blouses, and shoes. However, while they felt familiar, she couldn't remember events where she had worn them. There was nothing in the closet to be worn at a funeral, though Ava wasn't sure that she could still fit into the earlier clothes.

She pushed the older clothes out of the way and hung up her current clothes. Her outfits for the trip were mostly black since she had no idea if there would be a wake, a visitation, or just a funeral. The family had been tight-lipped about the schedule.

Her mother called from downstairs. Before she could respond, Donna shouted again. She remembered that tactic from her youth. Her mother made the second call fall almost at the end of the first so Donna could chide her children for being slow and lazy. So many times, she'd heard that speech about her lack of enthusiasm. Ava thought she could recite the lectures by heart—even now.

She made her way downstairs, deliberately taking her time. At the bottom of the stairs, Ava turned right and entered the kitchen. Her mother had made some sort of stew that looked like the recipe called for whatever was left in the fridge. She swallowed hard and took a seat.

Luke was not in the room. She wondered where he was.

"Took you enough time," Donna said with the same acerbic tone Ava remembered. The accusations. Ava was very aware that her mother had yet to welcome her to the house or mention her grandfather's demise. Ava felt weird, thinking so much had not changed in all these years. How could the world go on without this family changing?

"I'm just getting acclimated to the house," she said, trying to ignore the woman's behavior.

"If you came home more regularly, you wouldn't have that problem," her mother said. "We're still in the same place." Ava wasn't sure the statement was a positive.

"I'm doing very well in London, thanks."

Her mother just snorted and went back to the stove. With her back to Ava, she stirred the pot.

Ava could smell the aroma of freshly cooked bread. That was a different experience. Her mother's cuisine was usually any recipe that took less than three minutes to prepare with ingredients that could be found around the house. Her cooking skills leaned toward the convenient.

Ava looked at the place settings. She was shocked to see the blue ceramic cups they'd had as children. The blue ceramics were sitting on the table—one for her and one for Luke. Their names, in white letters, were on the side of the cups. The parents had not received similar cups.

Ava tried to recall when and how the cups had arrived at the house. She thought that her mother had ordered them, especially for the children, who had wanted toys and books for a present. Donna had thrown a fit when they were unappreciated.

Ava wondered why the cups had been brought out for this occasion. Indeed, after all these years, Luke still didn't drink out of the ceramic cup as he had as a child—or did he? The thought floored her. Luke was an adult. He should act like one.

Ava tried to put it out of her thoughts. Her mother was different. She'd known that since she was a small child. She would go to other children's homes, where their homes were quiet and tidy. Hers was not.

In part, at some point in her primary days, she'd known that her mother drank—heavily. She could be sweet and kind, but later, she would be forgetful and cruel on the same day.

As an older child, Ava had grown to have a wall around her. She had tried to shrug off her mother's behavior. Even when she was sober, her mother was slow, plodding in thought and unable to see the implications of a situation. Her mother had been more of a plow, pushing her way through any obstacles to get what she wanted.

The cups were a case in point, a less-than-subtle way to make Ava feel inadequate and unloving. She supposed a more loving child would have oohed and aahed over the handmade cups. Ava just wondered what her mother was up to.

Luke came in, and he poured two cups of bargain coke for them. Donna had always preferred water to sweet drinks, and

Ava could see the glass of clear liquid on the counter by the stove.

While Ava could feel her stomach was still rumbling, she wasn't looking forward to the meal. She'd really hoped that they would go out to dinner. She'd be fine with a simple fish and chips in town, but her mother had opted for a home-cooked meal instead. She would have to sneak out during the day to get a more nutritious meal for herself. Maybe she could convince Luke to go as well.

Luke sat down. Donna brought the stew to the table and set it down. She then brought her water glass to the table. Luke ladled out the stew to them and then ate quietly.

They all began eating, and Ava took a few bites. Then she happened to look down and found a dead fly in her stew. She picked it out and didn't eat anymore from that part of the bowl. The stew did not sit well with her. Ava's stomach churned as she finished the dish. She wondered about sneaking into York to get something else to eat. Now, it grumbled loud enough that the other two people looked up to see what was happening.

"Are you okay?" her mother asked, looking sad and concerned. It was Donna's first motion of concern, and Ava was immediately suspicious.

Ava had been sure that her mother was about to throw a fit and that her daughter had not appreciated the meal. She'd heard that lecture before—how hard she'd worked on the meal and how little her children enjoyed it.

"I'm just stressed and tired," Ava said, speaking over another rumble. The stew's taste came back into her mouth and burned her throat. She'd rarely had this sort of reaction to a meal in her years in London, but now it pained her.

"May I have some water?" Ava asked. She noted that she reverted to using the proper forms of may and can, the work of her mother, who screamed at them for their poor grammar.

However, Ava had to admit that proper grammar had served her well in London and the real estate office.

Her mother got up, found an empty glass, and filled it with tap water. Donna didn't say a word as she completed this request. She placed the cup on the table sharply, spilling a few drops around the glass.

Ava knew her mother was upset, but she couldn't help it. Taking the glass, Ava drank it down quickly. She had a few antacids in her bag. Still, leaving the table now, she would only receive more comments about her behavior and implied insults about her mother's cooking.

Ava took another sip.

"So, this is what life in London is like," Donna said. "You're so tense that you start vomiting up your food. You can't live like this. You should spend more time in York, where life is less stressful."

Ava started to protest, but her mother grew louder and spoke over Ava's words. She noticed that Luke seemed to shrink as their mother's voice became dominant. The screaming was giving her a headache, one that she didn't need with the growing belly pain.

"You just can't live like this. If you can't move back home, you should make more frequent trips. How do you think we feel when people ask where you are and how you are? We can't respond because you haven't been home in years. It's awkward. It makes us look like a dysfunctional family. It's embarrassing. Yet, you obviously don't care how I look. It's only you that matters."

Donna's outburst didn't make Ava want to visit more often. She was sure her stomach's protest indicated that she should cut them off entirely rather than come home to see her family. After all, she'd only come home for four days to pay her respects. Frankly, that seemed too long. She had work to attend to--another sale, perhaps. She had a busy social life that didn't involve this dreary house and the strange people who lived here.

Instead, she was sitting here and getting sick over her own set of nerves and whatever concoction her mother had served her. Ava was sensitive to some types of beans and grains, but she hoped her mother had recalled the sensitivities when making a meal. Perhaps that was too much to ask of her. Donna had not taken her daughter's ailments seriously.

"I'm going up to rest," Ava said. Granted, it was only the early afternoon, but she was worn out already. She left Donna carrying on with her diatribe.

The pain escalated as she walked up the stairs to her room. Ava looked in the medicine chest of the bathroom adjacent to her bedroom. Nothing in it would help a stomachache. She felt nauseous, and her memories came back of similar attacks when she was younger. Ava leaned over the toilet and stuck a finger down her throat.

The reaction was immediate. The stew from dinner and the drinks came up. She gagged and coughed, spitting out the last remnants of the meal. She put her hand under the tap and filled it with running water to rinse out her mouth. She spat it out and then rinsed the sink so her mother would find no sign of her activity.

If Donna realised what Ava had done, she would lash out, accusing her of illness and hating her cooking. Ava was there to remember her grandfather and not to get into another battle with her mother.

Chapter 4

The undertaker was adamant. "Miss, we don't have anyone here named Arthur Farley. We only have four clients currently, and I can assure you that none go by that name. I pride myself on knowing the families of each of our dearly departed guests."

Ava chewed on her nails. She could have sworn that her mother had given her this address for the funeral —and after all, how was it possible that she'd written down the wrong address when that address was also a funeral parlor? The incorrect address seemed unlikely to have taken her to another funeral parlor. The coincidence was too much.

Maybe she should have ridden with the others. Yet, she had wanted to be by herself to remember her grandfather's and honor his memory. Being with her mother and brother would have been chaotic. That was one of the reasons she had rented a car here in York. She had wanted the freedom to do as she pleased here, unlike the days of her youth. If the family got to be too much, she could always make a break for it.

Ava was frustrated. She was certain that her mother had given her this address. Yet, she saw no signs of any members of the family here. So, if she was the only one to have it wrong, could she have possibly written it down wrong? Ava hated this second-guessing herself. She had managed a thriving career in London, yet her time in York made her feel inadequate. She hated the feeling and right now, she hated York.

The undertaker cleared his throat. "I believe the funeral parlor you want is Crowley and Sons. It's about ten miles from here."

Ava gave him a raised eyebrow to express her doubts about his sudden answer.

"While we were talking, I texted a few other funeral directors in town. Old Mr. Crowley responded and said that the funeral is at his location." The undertaker gave her directions for the correct funeral parlor.

Ava fished for her keys in her jacket. The car key was crammed down in a small hole in the pocket. She cursed aloud, not worrying about what the funeral director would think. She bought this jacket two weeks ago, and now it had these little holes. The keys were stuck under the jacket lining, and Ava had to spend precious time pulling the keys out.

Ava remembered the holes from her youth—most likely a product of her mother's housekeeping. The holes were either the product of moths or mice. She shivered, thinking about rodents walking through her brand-new clothes and chewing holes in them. For all her claims of being a wonderful mother, Donna did not keep the house clean and pest-free.

She pulled her keys out, ripped the cloth, and made the hole larger than it had been. She cursed again, but now she was inside the car, and no one could hear her language. She started on the trip to the funeral parlor. The car's clock read 11 am, the time of the visitation and service at the funeral parlor. She was going to be late for the service. She could hear the recriminations from her mother now—and maybe even from Aunt Vicki if she was still alive.

Ava pushed down on the accelerator and began to make better time. However, when she'd almost made the halfway mark, the traffic slowed to a stop. Her phone indicated that a wreck had occurred two miles down the road, which meant that it could be up to an hour or more before she made it to her grandfather's service.

Ava looked at the side of the road and decided to take a risk. After all—while she had her license—she had never used it in London, where there were all tubes and taxis. A ticket or two would not damage her insurance prices, and she could always blame the London traffic for any aggressive driving.

She maneuvered the car into the bicycle lane and prayed that no one was out for a bicycle ride that day. The lane was clear as far as she could see, and she hit the accelerator. The car made a nasty noise, and Ava had a moment of panic. She envisioned her car dying in the bike lane, where she was sure to be caught.

The two miles went quickly, and she pulled out of the lane. Back on the road, she made the few remaining turns and pulled into the funeral home's carpark.

The service had not begun. Ava tried to tweak her appearance, wanting the family to see her in the best possible light after so many years. Even so, the attack of nerves the previous evening had left its toll on her. Ava had always felt that her nerves went right to her stomach. She looked pale, and Ava had eaten little. No one would think she was healthy and happy.

Her brother was outside the building, smoking. She had not been aware that he was a smoker. When did that start? He nodded as she came by.

"They're waiting on you," Luke said without emotion. He reached into his pocket and pulled out a flask. "You might need this. I know I will."

Ava knew he was likely right, and she twisted off the lid. The alcohol burned down her throat, reminding her of last night. She took another sip and handed it back to her brother. The warmth of the spirit would help her.

"Ready to go in?" she said.

Luke didn't look like he wanted to go. Ava wondered if he

had not had a good relationship with his grandfather in the past few years. He appeared to be sullen and withdrawn. What had happened here while she was gone?

They walked into the building. Even though Ava assumed that Luke knew the way, she had to lead them into the correct space. Perhaps he'd had too much of the flask.

People were milling around and talking to each other. Ava recognised a few as friends of her mother and neighbours who had lived near them for decades. However, there were far fewer attendees than Ava had expected. At one point, her grandfather had been known throughout York, and now he had been largely forgotten.

The conversation stopped when Ava and Luke entered the room. Donna started to come toward them, but Ava ignored her mother. Instead, she went to the coffin and looked at her grandfather for the first time in ages.

He looked much like he had the last time she'd been home. His face was peaceful. Someone had replaced the dark sunglasses he always wore on his face. Ava couldn't remember when she hadn't seen his face covered with the familiar, dark glasses. Day or night, light or dark, he always wore them. Ava had been convinced for years that he had a vision problem, but others assured her that it was just a quirk.

From her standpoint, she could see no signs of death. She wondered for the first time what had happened to him. Of course, he was pushing eighty, but old age was not a cause of death by itself. There had to be an underlying cause. She trusted no one there to tell her what had happened.

Donna didn't seem to mind that her daughter was sharing a moment with her grandfather. She then marched up to her and began to shout. "Where have you been? You do realise that you're late for the funeral. We had to wait, and of course, that would cost more money. Maybe you should pay for this, considering you couldn't think of anyone else today. You've always been selfish and inconsiderate. This is my father we're burying today." Donna broke into a loud sob that Ava suspected wasn't real.

She wasn't surprised. Ava should have known that her mother would try to pawn some of the costs of the funeral on her—and everyone else. No matter how much her grandfather had left them, the amount would not be enough for her mother. Even if her father had left everything to her, Donna would not be satisfied.

Ava clenched because Aunt Vicki approached her. If one was bad, two were worse. The sisters seemed to play off each other, a team of hate and malice that worked as one. Vicki was dark-haired with no signs of grey, even though she had to be sixty or more, and her dark brown eyes watched Ava as if she wanted to pounce. The woman had grown thicker since she'd last seen her, but Ava would not say that, no matter how bad the attacks would be. Vicki's outfit was an oversized black and white dress. It looked more like a dress for a dinner party than a funeral. Ava wasn't sure if that was the look Vicki had intended.

"You're late. Don't you ever consider anyone else but yourself?" Vicki said loud enough for the rest of the guests to hear. She pulled back the little black veil that hung to one side of her hat. "We should have left you in London."

Donna had stopped crying long enough to join the attack. "Never. She has always put herself first. It doesn't matter that the rest of us would like to pay our respects."

"She's going around the twist; she's a piece of work. A nasty piece of work. Always got to do one better than everyone else," Vicki said. "Never thought how all this was for your mother, and you didn't even show up on time." Vicki had probably been saving that for just such an occasion. "Even as a child, she never thought of anyone but herself. As soon as Ava could, she left and never came back. When her grandfather needed her most, she didn't come home. So typical of the bitch."

"You may be right about her mental state. It's never been quite right. If she gets nervous, she runs to the bathroom and throws up. She's an adult and can't handle the simplest suggestion for better behavior. It's disgusting," Donna said, providing an audience to her sister's accusations. They always worked as a team, agreeing with each other in their accusations. Ava wondered if they'd been born this vicious or had learned it, practicing on each other in their youth. "She's always seemed a bit off. She needs medical help if you ask me."

The funeral director cleared his throat. While Ava was sure that he'd witnessed families misbehaving in the past, she wanted no part of this drama. "May we get started?" His voice was calm as if this was merely a party for the deceased rather than a visitation for their grandfather.

Ava chose to sit several rows back from the rest of the family. That way, no one could watch her or make faces, as they'd be expected to look toward the front to the service going on.

At the end of the service, a song began to play. Ava wondered what music would have been chosen for her grandfather until it started playing. She was surprised when she recognised it to be the Birdie Song by The Tweets. This was an incredibly inappropriate song for a funeral, and everyone looked around at one another with a confused expression. The song gave the service an awkward feeling.

When she looked back at Donna, her mother smirked, shrugged her shoulders, and raised her hands. "It was his favorite song," Donna said.

Ava couldn't remember anything about her grandfather or

this song, and no one in her family was aware of this.

The service ended quickly. Ava had the distinct impression that the man had never met her grandfather. His words seemed to be platitudes rather than actual comments about Arthur Farley. The same speech could probably be given about any client at the funeral parlor. How well did anyone know her grandfather? Ava wondered again what happened to him over the years. Why was he no longer respected and honored like he had been years before? Had he done something to be excluded from society? Ava would like to know, but no one in the family would talk that candidly about him.

For a lifetime of living in York, few people were at the service. Ava had not expected hundreds of mourners today, but by her count, there were about twenty-five people in attendance. Ava supposed that the years had taken their toll; the friends her grandfather had shared years ago were no longer with him. He'd been trapped in the house those last few years, unable to drive or walk alone.

When the service finished, Ava was one of the first out of the door. She caught Luke as he came out of the building. "Fancy a ride?" she asked. At least if Luke were on her side, she wouldn't be lost or late. She wasn't going to have another scene like that. Luke didn't answer, but he followed her to the car park where the rental was still sitting.

Before she and Luke could leave, Donna stopped in front of them. She threw a handful of business cards for the funeral at Ava. "There. So, you won't have to lose the address next time — I'm sure you won't even bother to come to my funeral. Just throw me in a hole and be done with it."

She tramped away to her car. Donna turned and shouted, "Luke, you're going with me. Now. I don't want to hear any arguments from you."

Luke looked at his sister and then his mother before turning

31

and moving towards his mother. Ava would be alone again on this ride. She leaned over and picked up the business cards rather than seeing them left on the ground. Ava studied the cards for a minute. The address was nothing like the street and number she'd been given. What was happening here?

Chapter 5

Ava left the graveside service as fast as she could to avoid any more confrontations with her family. She wanted to process her feelings about being late, her mother's behavior, and her grandfather's death. She realised that she would only have had to deal with the latter in a more functional family. But this wasn't such a family.

Returning to the house, she went to her bedroom and stayed there, trying not to make any noise – or draw any attention. This was a strategy she had learned as a child. The less noise, the less chance of being the victim of her family's tongue-lashings. Downstairs, she could hear her mother and Vicki laughing—not the sounds of a wake for their father. Her grandfather had been a difficult man, rude and quick to snap at someone, but he was also kind at times and thoughtful of the family. It was one reason that Ava was surprised that he'd not made a will, instead leaving everything to his daughters —and with the taxes that came with a lack of instruction.

Ava waited until she was sure the others had gone to their rooms for the evening, to go downstairs and get something to eat. She was starving, but her need for food was less pressing than her need to be away from the others.

She found the bread and located some questionable deli meat. She thought about getting some decent food but was tired and ill-dressed in her black garment. When she finished making the sandwich, she took it upstairs to eat. Ava was still a bit unnerved by the holes in her clothes and likely vermin in the house. How could her mother have let the house get so rundown? Yet she recalled the same thing that happened to her as a child.

The light under Luke's door shone bright as she returned to her room. Ava decided to knock on his door and chat. Maybe Luke could explain what was going on around here.

Ava knocked on the door. No one answered. She tried knocking again, but there was still no response. She set her plate with the sandwich on the floor and tried the knob. It turned easily. "Luke," she said in a half-whisper. "Luke, mind if I come in?"

He did not respond, and Ava pushed the door open. Luke's room had the same creepy aura as her own. Luke had to be thirty-five now, but his room was still decorated in the same style as when he was a teenager. Why had he kept this décor?

The walls had football posters of players who no longer scored for any team. Luke had never been interested in sports, but her parents had forced Luke to play rugby and football. She remembered Donna accusing Luke of being a shame to the entire family.

The posters had the same torn and dusty look as the ones in her room. Luke had a twin-sized bed with a duvet featuring cars and trucks. Nothing in the room looked like it had been purchased in the last ten years. Was her family that poor, or did Luke fancy keeping the mementos of his childhood?

Luke looked asleep on the bed, though his long, lanky frame hung over on the sides and foot of the bed. That couldn't be comfortable. His neck curved back, and his long dark hair covered his eyes.

Ava decided to snoop a bit. She hadn't talked to her brother in ages and knew little about his life. First, she shut the door so Donna would not be tempted to barge in and accuse her of anything else.

She started the computer and began to scan his emails.

There was nothing of interest there. Most of the messages were junk, and it didn't appear that he looked at his email often. Due to work and friends, Ava couldn't go for a day without checking the various messages she received. Ava was sure that her mother frequently checked the machine for anything that might not meet her unspoken rules. Luke would have more freedom in prison than here.

She wondered if Luke had a mobile. She hadn't seen him use one, and she didn't see any indication of one on the desk or bed. It would be helpful if she could text him if she needed anything or just wanted to chat. She would have to ask him about it later. If he had any sense, it would be locked away in a lockbox inside a safe where only he knew the combination.

She studied Luke for a second on the bed. He looked less miserable when he was asleep like this. However, something was not right about his rest. She looked at him again, studying him more closely.

His chest was not making the typical up-and-down breathing motions. She could see the very light inhalation of his body, but the motion seemed odd—not the way that she breathed or the way the rare stay-over male friend breathed.

Ava became disturbed as she watched him breathe. Slowly, she made her way over to the bed. His upper arm was lying over the side of the bed, and she leaned down to check his pulse. It was weak and erratic, though his skin was still warm.

What worried her far more than his vital statistics was the empty bottle of pills on the bedside next to Luke. She didn't recognise the name of the pills, but she recognised what had happened in his room. Luke had attempted suicide.

After calling 999 and waiting by the front door for the ambulance, Ava was shocked that her mother had not come out to learn what the commotion was about. She could not carry Luke down the steep stairs to the ground level, so her best bet was to wait to see the emergency vehicles approach the house. She didn't need a jacket in the warm night air, and she paced back and forth on the path, hoping for the ambulance to hurry up.

As soon as the sirens came down the street, she waved her hands and motioned for them to pull into the drive. The two men took a stretcher up the stairs and quickly came back down with Luke's limp body.

She was relieved to see that Luke was hooked up to various machines and devices—and he was not covered by a sheet like she so often saw in the movies. He was alive.

The man who pushed the stretcher into the back of the ambulance looked at her and told her the name of the hospital Luke was being transported to.

Ava jumped into her rental and followed the ambulance as best she could. The hospital was familiar, but it had been years since she'd had to navigate York alone. She'd wanted Luke to help direct her movements from the funeral home. Now, sadly, he was.

She had to wait in the A & E waiting area as Luke was taken back to a room to pump his stomach in an attempt to revive him. Ava was fine staying here, not wanting to see that type of rescue.

A nurse came out of the room and invited Ava to come back. "Are you the only family?" she asked.

"Pretty much," Ava said, not wanting to get into the details of the situation. Ava was painfully aware that no one would be there for her in London. She would only have a boyfriend and no one else if she were lucky.

"Has he ever had depression or suicidal thoughts?" The woman took out some papers and started writing on them. "Does he have a history of contemplating suicide? Are there any drugs on your list that could cause suicidal thoughts or actions?"

"We buried our grandfather today," Ava said with a sigh. "He didn't seem to be overly upset at that time. He didn't cry or make any threats. As for the rest, I haven't seen him in years, so I can't answer those questions."

"So, there are signs of family separation. I'll make a note of that. Well, a psychologist will be coming in shortly, but until then, you may stay with him. It would probably be for the best. He'll be disoriented when he wakes." Before Ava could answer, the woman left the curtained room.

Luke made a noise and leaned forward to look at her. "You weren't supposed to do that. I didn't want to live." The hospital gown wasn't tied well, and the cotton fabric slid down his arm.

Ava went to the chair nearest to the bed and sat down. "Why? I know that things are not good at home. How could they be? Mum is a mess."

Luke laughed a hard, brash chuckle. "I wish that's all it was. She's the least of my problems."

Ava started to ask and then stammered. She had no right to ask him anything about his most personal decisions. She had not been here.

It couldn't have been easy, still living in a two-decade-old set of memories in his room. She had not helped him. She'd been making her own life in London.

"We were abused," Luke said. In the silence, the words seemed to echo.

Ava paused and looked at him. Luke had said "we," as in her participation was included.

"What did you just say?" Ava asked, thinking that she might have misheard her brother.

"We were abused—physically, emotionally, and sexually," he said again.

Ava took a deep breath. "I wasn't abused. I don't remember

that."

"I do," Luke said softly. "Touching me. A dark space. Forcing me to do things." He made a sound that Ava suspected was crying, but she didn't turn to look at him. Her heart was already breaking for him.

"Did you tell the doctor about this?" Ava asked.

Luke nodded. "I had to tell him. It feels like it's all going to burst out of me. I've held it back for so long—this is what happens."

"How old were you?" Ava asked. She was trying to find the timeline for this tragedy. Had she been around then, or had she already left for London and better memories? How could she have missed seeing this happen to Luke? Or had she known what was happening and tried to put on blinders so she couldn't see what was happening?

"I think I was about seven or eight. Why?" Luke shifted to sit up in the bed. It clearly took him more effort to move. His body didn't seem to be his.

"I'm just wondering where I was. If I saw this?" Ava calculated that she had to be around ten or eleven years old. Primary school was too early to process what was happening, but then it was also too early to be the victim of abuse.

"Ava, it's not like they put out signs to tell everyone. They were secretive about the whole thing. No one caught on to what they did."

Ava shuddered. Luke had said "they," presumably meaning that more than one person had abused him. She couldn't get her mind around the situation. Luke was saying that he'd been abused by multiple people, and she hadn't seen or remembered the signs of this heinous crime. Was he telling the truth, or was he so far gone into the nasty world of her mother that he believed anything she said? Ava knew her mother's overbearing personality could steamroll the strongest people. No telling what she could have done to a young boy. Donna had always had a firmer grip on Luke than Ava. Even if Ava hadn't known about this, her mother had to realise what was happening to Luke. If nothing else, he'd been out of the house for long periods. Hadn't she been responsible for the welfare of her children?

The doctor came in again. "I'm checking in on my patient," he said with what was obviously a fake smile. "I'm thinking of releasing you, Luke, but I'll need to be assured that you won't be alone. Get dressed." Luke walked slowly, with a shuffling gait, to the bathroom and closed the door.

He turned to Ava. "You're the one who found him, right? You're the sister? Can you stay with him for a few days? He needs care, and he needs someone to watch over him— he may try to do this again. I'd feel much better if I knew that you were going to be there."

Ava stammered. She hadn't planned on staying more than another night, but the doctor was discussing several days. She wondered if she could get a few more days off from work. It would be costly for her, missing work and the opportunities that came with additional sales, but it was for Luke.

A flash of anger welled up in her. She knew that neither her mother nor Luke would come running to take care of her. She'd be lucky to get as much as a card from them, and here, the doctor wanted her to stay with Luke and play nurse for an undetermined amount of time. When had Luke ever been nice to her? Ava's memories of her brother recalled that he'd been nasty to her, teasing her, calling her names, and hiding or breaking her few possessions.

Before she could say anything else, Luke came from the loo wearing the same clothes he'd had on earlier, the suit trousers, the white shirt—which now had vomit on it—and dress shoes without socks. It was a brutal reminder that she'd been at the funeral just before this happened.

Ava thought again about Luke's actions. Had he been so close to his grandfather that he decided he couldn't live without him? That seemed unlikely from Ava's perspective. Her grandfather had been crusty, sullen, and not personable. She couldn't see anyone making a deep connection with him.

She nodded, and the doctor pulled out a wad of forms and a pen. After reading the papers, Ava signed them. Her years in the real estate industry had taught her to read carefully. Ava finished the forms and handed them back to the doctor.

They were going home.

Chapter 6

When they arrived home, the house was still quiet. Her mother had missed all the excitement. She hadn't called the hospital, and now she was not sitting up waiting for them. Ava helped Luke get into his room and then left him. When she closed the door, he was stripping out of the suit trousers and getting into bed. She hoped they were good for the night.

The events had shaken her. Even though it was after three in the morning, Ava couldn't sleep. The sight of Luke lying on the bed and the revelations about the reason for his suicide attempt. Was any of that true? At the least, he believed it strongly enough that he'd tried to do away with himself. She hoped for his sake that it had been a product of the pills and emotional distress, but somehow, she didn't think that was true. Luke had been abused as a child, and she hadn't known about it.

Ava pushed the pillows up against the headboard and sat there to think. Perhaps the quiet time would give her some insight into Luke's behavior over the years. He had been moody, distant, and always confrontational. Life in her family—as a child or now as an adult—had not been easy.

Sometime during the short night, Ava slipped into slumber, and her neck ached when she arose. She'd slept for hours in the awkward position of sitting up against the wooden headboard. She got up slowly and tried to relieve the tension in her neck by rotating it in all directions. A few pops and all was well. She wished that everything could be fixed so easily.

Her mind drifted back to last night, and Ava began to think

about the time with Luke. What had he been doing? Why would he want to kill himself? She went to the Bathroom, shook her head and splashed some water on her face. She had tried to get him to talk last night, but he'd been too out of it.

Now, she worried about the doctor's request that she watch him for a few days. She felt guilty for wanting to return to her nice, normal life. She had not missed this drama and confrontation at all. Her mother was always like this. She didn't know how people could live in this maelstrom of emotions and angst.

She went downstairs to scrounge for something to eat. Donna was a rubbish cook and probably had nothing edible in the fridge. The shelves were barren. Goodness knows she tried, but her mother found the most improbable recipes in the local papers and tried them out on her children.

However, Ava was in luck. Half a dozen eggs and a few containers of yogurt had not gone off yet. She sat back to eat a cherry yogurt while she read the news on her phone. Most of the information regarded London, and again, she was struck by how vibrant that city was in comparison to the drab feeling of York. In fairness, Ava had to assume that many negative emotions towards the town came from her family.

She cleaned the kitchen and put away the dishes, which didn't appear to be done often. Ava even cleaned the ugly blue ceramic cup with her name on it. She was tempted to break it in the sink but chose not to. She had enough battles with her mother at the moment. She looked at the time and decided to call her office and ask for a few more days off. She couldn't leave Luke like this, even if no one in her family would do this for her.

Donna walked in as Ava moved to go upstairs. She looked around at the now-cleaned kitchen and gasped. "You can't leave good enough alone. You have to be doing something to show you're better than me. Always the snob. Make the house look 'presentable."

Donna was carrying an armful of paperwork, and a few sheets fell to the floor. Ava leaned down to pick them up. The papers dealt with estate and property distribution. These had to be her grandfather's papers regarding his death. Ava felt slightly sick to her stomach, thinking that her mother had started working on the matter so soon after the funeral. Grandfather wasn't even cold in his grave, and Donna had started collecting the money and the house. Ava had been told repeatedly as a girl that her grandfather was quite well-off, but no one had ever put a hard number on his wealth. Rich was such a subjective term.

As an adult, Ava had no idea where the funds had come from. She could not recall her grandfather ever working for a living. Granted, in his later years, he lived on pensions and such, but what had he done for a living—and how had he become so wealthy?

"What are you looking at?" Donna snarled. "I have lots to do here. Think you're getting a piece of this? Not while I'm around, you're not. Every last penny was left to me, and only me."

Ava handed the papers to her mother. "They're not hard to fill out. I do it all the time." She shrugged as she started to leave.

Donna grunted. Ava realised that her mother would never politely ask her for help. That would make her look weak and inferior to Ava. She was too proud for that. Despite Ava's success in London, she would always be inferior to her mother, according to Donna. The notion made her pause. What a horrible thing to think—that Ava was beneath her in every way! No wonder she had some issues with self-esteem and her worth.

Ava took a few pages and smoothed them out on the table.

"See, this one, you just need to sign here. There are no requirements for witnesses or a notary. These require two witnesses who are not related to you. Could you ask a neighbour or a friend?"

Ava wasn't sure if her mother had any friends or congenial neighbours. It had been so long since she'd seen Donna socialise with others. Donna had focused on her father, her sister, and the children for years—even now, Donna did the same thing. She focused on Luke and her father's health until he passed away. And then there was one...

Ava quickly sorted the estate papers into categories based on the type of signature needed. The stack of sheets that only required to be signed by one person was handed to Donna to sign.

"Does Aunt Vicki need to sign these too?" Ava asked. She wasn't sure how the will was structured – if both women, the only two remaining heirs, would receive equal amounts or if another set of bequests were included. Her grandfather would be the type to pit the two women against each other with an unequal will. However, Donna had been adamant that the estate was hers. Was that true?

"She does, but I can sign for her," Donna said. Donna took the pen and signed in another manner that appeared to be another's signature. Ava wondered where her mother had learned that.

In the law, Donna couldn't sign for her sister unless she had a power of attorney for the woman. With that type of power, Vicki would not trust her sister, not anyone. The family had no trust or reliance on each other. Even then, she should have signed her own name, followed by the initials of power of attorney. However, it looked as though Vicki had signed her own name.

Ava was leery of her mother's antics. Minor issues like this likely meant that Donna had more extensive schemes in the background. Ava hoped to be gone before any ramifications of her stunts became public. Donna could be vicious when crossed.

With that, Ava got up and left to return to her room. She did not want to see her mother forge the paperwork to cash in on her father's estate. Ava still had to make that call to her work. Another four days would ensure that Luke was well enough to be left unattended. She could count the hours until she could go home.

She dialed her boss at the real estate agency and waited for him to answer. The call went to voice mail.

She wasn't sure what troubled her. Instead of a four-day holiday, Ava asked for two weeks off. When she hung up, she looked at herself in the mirror. What had Ava done? She had trapped herself in a house with Donna, Luke, and an occasional visit from Vicki, who yelled at her and hated her. She couldn't imagine the hell it would be to stay another fortnight with them.

She went to Luke's room to check on him. The door was open; that had been a requirement for Ava. She didn't want to embarrass Luke in any way, but she needed to be able to check on him at any time. He was sitting on the bed cross-legged. He hadn't bothered to wear a t-shirt last night, and Ava tried her best not to stare at his hairless, childlike torso. Even his body made him look like a younger man who was dominated by his mother.

Across his chest, he had cut himself multiple times, enough to show the marks on his skin. He also had a series of tattoos across one shoulder. Some images were clearly professional, while others had been carved into his skin by an obvious amateur.

He was playing a game on his phone. Ava could hear the

sounds of weapons firing. Luke didn't even bother to look up when she entered. She only stayed long enough to see that he was alive and breathing.

She went back downstairs to find her mother reading paperwork at the table. "Do I really need Vicki to sign these?" she asked. Ava looked at the woman. Sometimes, she suspected that her mother was not all there. The question regarding legality should have been easy to comprehend. Still, her repeated question was too far over her head. Ava had always felt compelled to explain things two or three times to get her mother to understand what was being said.

"If you want them to be legal, you do." Ava pointed out that the papers needed to be signed in blue ink because they were reproduced more visibly. She ran back up to her room, where she had a stack of pens in her bag. She brought those down and hoped she didn't have to make any more trips up and down the stairs.

While getting her mother set up with the papers and a notary to come to the house the following day, Ava thought the moment was what she'd hoped for her entire life. A family that could sit down and discuss work and life without yelling, screaming, and recrimination.

By the time they finished the paperwork, Ava had reduced the number of papers to a handful, with those being cared for by the notary. Ava had printed a few extra copies of some documents, hoping she could convince her only to sign her own name on the paper.

As she sat in her mother's house and talked to Donna, she was surprised at how peaceful it was. Was Donna using her for her real estate skills, or was this actually a moment of a quiet truce between them?

Chapter 7

After a few days of putting together the paperwork for her mother, Ava decided to take some time for herself. Most of her friends had left York years ago, and she missed the camaraderie of work. She had tried to reach out to a few secondary school friends for a gathering, but they were spread all over Britain and Europe.

Still, Ava managed to find two friends in town, and together, they decided to go to The Swan, a pub near Ava's mother's home. The old pub had been a hang-out in secondary school, as the pub had not bothered to check IDs for the students.

"You won't get lost that way," Sally said. "You've been gone for ages."

Maria posted a laughter emoji as well. "It'll be good to see you," she texted.

Ava received another message from Mrs. Horridge, the teacher she'd seen on her first day here. The woman kept sending texts that seemed to be urgent. Ava couldn't imagine what that earth-shattering thing could be after all this time, so she had not bothered to reply yet.

They met the following Friday night. The week had been quiet. Donna seemed to be busy with the contents of her father's house.

The bar looked nothing like it had twenty years ago. Then, it had been a hard-drinking bar where people came to get drunk—and students came to try the forbidden liquids. Now, the bar had that ambiance of an English pub, but not a real pub, more like the pub she would see in a movie. The wooden sign with the title and some faded food on the plaque was over the front door. Ava felt momentarily uneasy as she walked into the pub as if danger was behind the door. However, she couldn't remember any specific problems with this place.

When she went inside the area for drinkers and diners, it was mixed with the tables for eating on the right side of the space and the drinkers on the left. They achieved this by putting a large wooden bar and stools there. Many of the offerings were stereotypes of what she would expect. British brews alongside a few Irish and Scottish brands as well. Ava had been spoiled with the number of London bars that sought trendy drinks rather than trying to impress tourists.

Ava had arrived before her two friends, so she got a Guinness and decided to find a table where they could talk without interruptions. The drink had been her grandfather's favorite, and she fondly remembered him allowing her a sip of the stout when she was younger.

She found a table in the front corner of the bar and sat down. Before she could even take her first sip of her stout, two men had approached her to offer a drink—or more. She declined both offers.

Maria arrived first. The room seemed to light up as she came in. The men stopped to look at her, with her raven-dark hair and black eyes. She was bewitching, with a slight bounce to her step that made her look happy and vibrant. Ava had always been slightly jealous of her friend's exuberance. She could never be that happy all the time.

"Ava!" she shouted about the chatter of the patrons and the noise of the 80s songs. "How are you?"

She gave Ava a bear hug. Ava reciprocated and then stopped. She could see Luke at the other end of the bar from a distance. He was with two people, a couple, she surmised. The woman kissed the other man a few times. She wished that she could hear what they were saying.

Luke looked animated, almost a different person than he'd looked like before. The man looked familiar, and Ava wondered if he, too, was here hanging out with friends. The man was probably not much older than Luke, though he clearly worked out. His stance was firm, and the muscles in his short-sleeved shirt nearly broke their stitches. The woman was attractive in a generic way. She was blonde, clearly from a bottle, with a spray tan and a dress that Ava would not have dreamed of wearing.

Then the man gave Luke money, a roll of cash secured by a rubber band. Luke didn't bother counting the cash, which suggested this was not a legitimate business transaction. He stuffed it in his pocket and smiled again. Ava couldn't believe that this was the same man who had wanted to end his life a few days earlier. How much booze had he downed so far—to be this friendly?

She wondered about the roll of cash, too. Was Luke involved in drugs in some way? If he was, the money indicated that he was selling it, not just using it. That might explain his suicide attempt and his desire to cover up the drug trafficking by using child abuse instead. Luke had some secrets that Ava knew nothing about.

Maria cleared her throat loudly. "Ahem, did I bore you already?" she asked. "Please don't tell me the night is over?"

Ava shook her head and focused her thoughts again. "No, I just saw Luke, and I'm surprised. He has been so down lately, and now he is in good spirits. I was trying to figure out what happened in between."

Maria spun around and stared until Ava tapped her shoulder. "Sorry, now I guess I was lost for a minute too. I wouldn't have known Luke. He looks nothing like he did in secondary school." Maria remembered some things about Ava's brother, such as his academic career and personality. Her tone suggested that she might be interested in Luke from secondary school. Still, Ava didn't recall any of her friends being interested in her brother.

"I see him in here occasionally, but he's always with someone—usually someone different, sometimes men and sometimes women. I would never have known that he was Luke Hedges. Fancy that."

Originally, Ava had thought about asking her about Luke and the abuse. However, when she sat at the table, she knew she couldn't do it. She was here to get away from the stress of her home, and it would violate Luke's privacy. Both seemed like good reasons to let it go for the night.

She decided to tell her just enough to see if it would bring up any details. "Luke is not like that today," Ava said. She went on to tell Maria that Luke had been to the hospital—she thought she had said nothing about his claims.

"Don't you believe him?" Maria started, but a new voice interrupted them.

"Ladies!" Sally said, shouting above the noise that had become even more raucous than in secondary school. "It's so good to see you!"

The previous topic was forgotten. When Ava looked over again, Luke and his friends had left the bar. She had no idea when he'd left—or whether he had seen her or not.

"So, tell us what you've been up to," Sally started.

Fortunately for her, Maria decided to go first and gave a lengthy story of her love life and two divorces.

The entire situation sounded messy, with the multiple children by different husbands. By the time she was done, Ava was almost happy to be staying with her mother and brother. It sounded like a much smoother time.

Maria looked at Ava and said, "It's your turn. I've wanted to hear everything about you since we got here. What's new with you?"

Ava's story sounded dull, even to her. She'd gone to London, lived in a flat with a roommate, had a dry spell of selling real estate, and had returned to York to help her family after her grandfather's death.

Maria smiled at Sally. "You should see her brother. He's a bit dodgy, but he's hot."

Sally looked around, wanting to see Luke, but he had left earlier. She sighed and turned to the others. Her story was less adventuresome than Maria's tale. However, it was along the same lines. Sally had married once and now had four children by the same man. She complained for twenty minutes about his faults as though she had memorised a list of shortcomings.

By the time she was done, Ava was happy that she wasn't seeing anyone seriously. The manager at the real estate company flirted with her at times, and she'd had a few dinner dates that had gone nowhere.

"Didn't you get some of your grandpa's money?" Maria asked. "I thought that's why you were here. That would mean Luke wouldn't need to be doing whatever he's doing, right?"

Ava told them the story, and both women seemed disappointed by the news. Sally looked puzzled. "Old Horridge told us that you were going to be rich. Now you have to rely on finding a rich husband like the rest of us."

Ava assured her that no wealthy man was in her life.

Sally was aghast when she heard this, which might have been exacerbated by the third mojito. "We have to change that!"

Maria seconded the idea. "What's your type?" she asked. "Or does that matter if you'll only be here a few weeks? Mister Right Now could be here too."

Ava tried to change the subject, but they were having none

51

of that. They wanted to add their friend to the current pool of dating possibilities.

Sally jerked her head toward the bar. "Take a look at the man there. He's sort of hot."

Maria turned to look and then turned back. "Not him. Definitely not him. I went out with him twice. He wasn't worth the time or the effort. Next!"

Ava tried to explain to Maria and Sally that she had a boyfriend in London. Granted that Simon had missed her party in London, and he hadn't called back when she called to say she had to go out of town. Only a few nights later, he'd left a voicemail for Ava, telling her how sorry he was, and Simon hoped she would be back soon.

Ava was suspicious of the call. Simon once showed her how to send a message to someone else's voicemail while skipping the whole mess of dialing the number. Ava thought it was only a step above ghosting. In that manner, a person could leave a quick message and be done. No long chats or discussions were needed. So perhaps the women were right about Simon. He was nothing more than a short-term lover and not a long-term mate.

The women commented about various men at the bar and even a few men who were eating with a woman. Ava had to admit that the women were picky. They even excluded men who ate fish and chips or a dish they disliked.

Ava looked at the bar again, wondering when she could escape the booze-induced matchmaking. Maria looked over and pointed at the man at the bar. Ava had to admit that he was attractive. He had dark hair that was slightly longer than usual, with a few curls that hung down nearly to his deep blue eyes. He wore a shirt and tie, which made him stand out from the rest. He was muscular, and his shirt clung to his arms and chest.

He was standing next to two women, but his posture did not indicate interest in either one. He stood a short distance from them, looking as if he could run away when he wanted to.

"We have a winner!" Sally said. Ava shushed her, not wanting the man to look over and think that all three women were three sheets to the wind.

Maria shoved a twenty at Ava. "Buy us a round. Go to the bar, pick an open place next to him, and then chat with him while the bartender is busy."

The two women ordered complicated drinks containing multiple types of booze—Ava had never even heard of some of the mixtures.

She walked to the bar, turning around occasionally to check on her friends. It would be like them to skip out, leaving her with three drinks and no way to avoid this handsome stranger.

The bartender had heard of all the drinks, and he began mixing them. Ava watched him for a minute and then turned around again to check the table. In the process, she bumped into the man spotted by her friends.

"Excuse me," she said, turning back to the bar.

"Quite okay with me. Your friends are waving at you." The man had a nice smile and seemed cheery—not as bubbly as Maria, but friendly and warm.

Ava could have crawled out of the bar at that moment. She had spent years waiting for men to hit on her, not the other way around.

"I'm ignoring them. They see a good-looking guy, and they act like fifteen-year-olds."

"They think I'm good-looking?" he asked. The grin he flashed could almost be considered a smirk.

"I believe I said that they do," Ava replied, giving him a grin saying that she was onto his tricks.

"Well, if you're going to be that way, I won't tell you that I think you're a very attractive woman. Are you new to town? You seem a bit awkward here, but at the same time, you're here with friends, which makes it seem like you've been here before."

Ava raised an eyebrow. "I will say that I admire your deductive powers. I lived here when I was younger, but I've lived in London for the past few years. And you? I don't recall you being here when I was in school, yet you seem about the same age as me."

"Since you asked, I'm thirty-seven, and you? I've been here six years in total, and I'm associated with the hospital in town. I grew up in Devon, which would explain why a local woman like you didn't go to school with me."

"How many of those bottles have you had, sir? You're asking a lady her age." Ava feigned a moment of indignation and then laughed.

"A very saucy humor," the man said. "I like that. May a gentleman ask your name."

"Ava, Ava Hedges. And you?"

"George Shaw." He held a hand out. She shook his hand, and the moment lasted slightly longer than she expected. There was just a hint of electricity and excitement that she hadn't expected. What was it with this man? He had a persona that Simon had never had.

"Nice to meet you," Ava said.

The bartender brought the three drinks and placed them on the bar before Ava. She paused for a second, not knowing how to handle the situation of taking the drinks to her friends — and yet not allowing this conversation to end. Ava had to admit that her friends were right. She needed this, and the spark between them was palpable.

"Why don't I help you?" George said and picked up a glass. "Then I can get your friends' approval for a proper date."

Ava tried not to smile. "Shouldn't you ask me first? After all, I am thirty-five."

Now, George gave her a grin. "So, you were right about the ages. Good detective work, Watson."

"Shouldn't I be Holmes?" Ava asked. She could feel her cheeks flush and her eyes sparkle. What was wrong with her that she couldn't keep the conversation to casual?

"I shall be Watson if you insist," George said, giving her a slight bow while not spilling a drink.

They took the glasses back to the table. Ava reclaimed her seat, and George brought another chair back to the table, where he sat next to Ava.

The table had been set up for three, meaning George was now much closer than before. At times, his arm or shoulder brushed against hers.

After finishing the round of drinks, Maria and Sally made excuses to leave. They promised to do this again soon. Sally gave her a quick wink and a smile.

"Well, your friends—very kindly—left us alone."

Ava sighed. "Yes, that was a rather obvious play on their part. Sometimes, I don't think they've grown up."

"Sometimes being young at heart is a good thing. It can keep you feeling healthy and engaged in the outside world. Other times, that attitude can be the cause of many issues. They do call it the Peter Pan syndrome for a reason. That refusal to never grow up."

Ava looked at him. "You're a psychologist, aren't you?"

He laughed. "You certainly should be Holmes after that deduction. Sorry, it's a habit. Did I start analysing your friends? And what do you do for a living?"

Ava told him about real estate and how she'd recently sold a house that she had not thought would be easy to sell.

"That's amazing," he started. Then he stopped. He pointed to a group of older women who were waving in his direction. "Those women over there are my ride. I'm going to have to leave. Could we exchange numbers? I'd like to see you again."

Ava tried not to pry, but everything in her wanted to scream about the fact that he was going home with them. "Sure."

"They're long-time friends. Nothing else. It's rather like your night out. You and two friends, me and two friends."

Ava smiled, relieved that he wouldn't be going home to spend the rest of the evening with the women, who were both attractive.

Ava was glad that Geroge walked her to her car. She hadn't lived here for years and had no idea if the streets were safe after dark.

They paused at her car, and George leaned in for a kiss. Ava was more than happy to move closer to him, allowing his lips to brush against hers. She felt that same thrill she'd experienced when they had first touched hands. George had a chemistry about him.

He leaned in further, and now his lips pressed against her with passion. Ava wanted him. She nearly stopped, thinking she sounded too much like her friends. It would be better to wait, especially given that she lived with her mother, who would end the moment upon their entry, and he had two friends with him.

He must have been thinking the same way since he pulled away in a few seconds, and Ava could hear his heavy breathing.

"I would like to see you again," George said.

Ava merely nodded her head. "Soon."

George got out his mobile and handed it to Ava to get her to enter her phone number. She felt electricity running throughout her body whilst punching in each number.

George smiled and walked back toward his car. His friends waved at Ava and then laughed. None of them had taken offense, so Ava presumed none of them were romantically involved. Given her recent experience with Simon, this pleased her.

Chapter 8

W hen she returned home, the lights were on under Luke's door again. Ava's first idea was panic. She had found him that way only a few days ago, but she still felt responsible for his attempt and her promise to the doctor to keep an eye on him.

She knocked on the door, but this time, Luke opened the door. "Yeah?" he said with a snarl.

"I was just checking on you...you know?" Ava said, trying not to mention the event by name and not talking about what Luke had said at the hospital.

"I'm alive," Luke said. He almost smiled at her. "Is that all you wanted to know?"

Ava looked at him, trying to decide if she should go on. "I saw you at the pub tonight. You were with some friends."

"You could say that," Luke said, rolling his eyes.

"They weren't friends?" she asked. Ava recalled the exchange of cash between them. Had Luke been buying drugs, or had he been selling?

"Come on. Just ask it. I can see that we weren't as discreet as we could have been."

Ava took a deep breath. "Well, it looked like you were buying drugs. After the way I found you, I was concerned you would take too many pills again. The doctor told me to keep an eye on you, and I am trying to follow his orders."

Luke looked at her and shook his head. "That was not a drug transaction. Far from it. Are you sure you want to go into this matter? You seemed fairly upset the other day when I mentioned it?"

"You mean the abuse? What did that have to do with those people? Are they therapists?" Ava couldn't make sense of what he was saying. These people were not old enough to have been abusers. So, what was he doing with them?

"They were definitely not therapists. Look, if you want to know, they weren't interested in drugs. They were interested in me." Luke didn't make eye contact after that. His head hung down, much like Ava had seen him on her first day in York.

"You sold yourself?" Ava asked. She couldn't believe what she was hearing. She had left a calm and peaceful life in London. Now she was home and finding out that her brother was selling himself.

"Yeah, once you get passed around as a kid, you don't worry too much about doing the same as an adult. Plus, the money is good. I have to work somehow, and the petrol station doesn't pay much."

Ava felt ashamed that she hadn't even known he worked at a petrol station. He had such potential as a kid, intelligent, friendly, and happy. Now he pimped himself out to make ends meet. Was this the result of the abuse, or were there other dark secrets that Ava didn't know about?

"Don't tell me my perfect sister doesn't remember any of this. You had this happen to you as well, but you could bounce back into York acting like nothing ever happened." Luke faced her now, and his face was reddening. "That makes the experience ten times more difficult. I don't have you on my side. You think I'm making it all up for attention—or what?"

"Those things didn't happen, though. I don't remember any abuse." Ava was getting frustrated with him. He insisted that she had the same memories, but nothing came to mind--even when she thought about her youth. "I'm certainly not conducting myself the way you are."

"I'll give you a starter. We were taken down to a room where you and I were abused. We weren't the only children. There were others. Plenty of others. And then other adults came and abused us. Not once or twice, but more times than I could count or want to count. It was disgusting. It's still disgusting when I see those people walking around York, and they nod at me as if we were acquaintances. Why can't you remember that? It was horrendous."

"Maybe that's why I don't remember those things. My brain doesn't want to process it."

Luke sighed. "Must be nice. Life would be better if I could forget what those people did to me. Why didn't I think of that? Now, if my brain would cooperate."

Ava nodded. "And that's why you do those things?" She still couldn't believe what her brother was doing. "Does Mum know about this?"

"Ava, I'm an adult male. I can do what I want and not do what I don't want. She doesn't know anything about what you do at night in London. I'm sure you have gentlemen friends over to your flat. She shouldn't know what I do here. Besides, she has her own issues right now. I'm sure you saw the work they've been doing on the house and all those forms."

Ava tried to talk more to Luke—to bring out these memories and perhaps talk him into some type of therapy, but he was having none of it. He didn't want his mother to find out. Ava was unsure why he felt that way. Donna had been supposedly responsible for them, hadn't she? Where had she been when Luke was taken to that place he had talked about?

Still, despite her worries, the evening had been long, and she'd had a few drinks. She needed some sleep before the new day started. She rested on her bed with the pillows pushed up against the headboard as she had the other night.

She lay back and closed her eyes.

In those moments before she fell asleep, she envisioned a dark room with a staircase leading up to the light. Ava snapped up and looked around her bedroom. Had she actually seen the place Luke had talked about—or was this only a matter of dreaming about something you heard? Ava had suffered a few nightmares after watching a slasher movie. Perhaps this was like that. However, Ava had not been asleep now; she had only been in the moments before sleep.

She wracked her brain, trying to think if she'd seen this image before, but it was new to her. There was one way to find out. She walked along the landing and opened Luke's door. "I need to talk," she said. Her vision of the place matched Luke's description exactly—as if perhaps Ava had just taken Luke's words and made them into an image.

Luke sat on the edge of the bed while he heard the description of the place Ava had seen. "That's it. You knew all this time and lied to me about it. That's cruel. Why would you lie? You're the only other person I know who went through this. We should be together—not apart."

"I didn't lie. It just happened—just now. The room, the darkness, the stairs on one side of the room. And I felt so many emotions there. It was like a nightmare."

"What color were the stairs?" Luke asked.

Ava knew he was skeptical after their earlier conversation, but it hurt that he didn't believe her.

"White, but chipped and dirty. Like they'd been there many years."

"Yeah, that's it. So, what else do you remember?" Luke asked, now interested in what his sister had to say.

"Not much. I just feel the emotions of being assaulted. I'm afraid and disgusted and know I'm doing wrong—even though I have no choice. It's disgusting."

"How long have you had these feelings?" Ava asked.

"Years. I think I started picking up on them right after secondary school. They didn't start with a vision of the room like you had. They were graphic, painful, disgusting. I saw it all. At first, I thought I was going crazy, seeing all these things about people I knew. But no matter what I did, the visions were there. The later flashbacks, they're called, built on the earlier ones, and by the time I saw a shrink, I could see about twenty people abusing me—and about a dozen kids being abused."

"Donna sent you to a psychologist?" Ava asked, feeling that her mother would never be that reasonable.

"Hardly," Luke laughed. "That's when I started making my own money. It was the only way to make enough money to see the shrink. She helped me understand what they were, but that was it. Nothing seemed to make them stop."

"That's been a long time. Did something trigger it that made it come to life?"

"Yeah. I'd been dating this girl for a while. We were getting serious. And there was this wall between us, a feeling that I could never be honest with her. She felt it—I felt it. Then we got—intimate, and it was nothing like I expected. I cried in the middle of it, and these memories kept flashing back to me afterward like someone had started a movie of these things that had happened to me. That's when I stopped dating and stopped hanging out with friends. If I needed money, I just got someone to pay for me. I felt better about that. I was making the choices."

"And you never mentioned this to me?"

"What was I supposed to say? 'Hey, sis, do you remember going into a cellar somewhere and being abused? There's no good way to start that conversation."

"You saw it as a cellar also?" Ava asked, thinking back to her memory. The dark space with the stairs up to the light.

"Yeah, I can see it clearly, but I have no idea where it's at. I can tell you it's not here or at grandfather's home either." Luke's voice had a catch in it. Ava looked for signs that he might start crying, but he swallowed hard and continued. "So, it was my secret. Mine alone."

"How could Donna let that happen? She must have known about it. We would be gone for a time—without her."

"Are you sure about that?" Luke asked. His tone was sharp like a whip. "I trust no one. I even suspected you for a while, but the more I thought about it, the less sense it made. So, you're the only one I can believe at this point."

Ava looked at him. "I'm not going to be like that. I can't be like that."

Luke shrugged. "At least you have a therapist now. Free tips on how to recover from abuse. Maybe he'll help you stuff all those memories back in the closet so you can go on being happy and lively."

Ava cringed. Word spread around quickly in York. She hated the thought that this might be true. She'd been abused before she was old enough to know what was happening—and she'd shoved it down so far into her memories that she didn't even recall them.

Without a word, Ava headed back to her room. She was scared. The first memories had come to her as she drifted off to sleep. She didn't want to have that experience again. It was too much for her.

Her eyes flickered, and the memory began again. The cellar was a clear memory. She could see the paint chips missing on the wall and the damp places along the floor. The scent was musty yet cold.

She tried to determine how old she was, but it wasn't clear. She wasn't yet a woman, so she guessed herself to be ten or maybe twelve, too young for this to happen.

She woke with a start and ran to the bathroom. She threw up twice before her stomach was empty, and the good times she had with George that evening were gone, replaced by the memories she was experiencing over and over.

She went back to her bed. Sleep came.

Chapter 9

Ava looked at the table, where four place settings were now set. She had invited George over. She had suggested the date at Donna's house, even though it seemed a little early in the dating process. George seemed fine with the invitation.

She smiles. George had sent roses and lilies, which spiced up the middle of the table and made it look more festive. She couldn't remember the last time she'd received flowers from an interested man—years, at least.

Her mother and Luke had not been thrilled with the announcement. For some reason, the people she had left here in York years ago were different now. They didn't want to socialise. Luke and her mother felt comfortable with their own company—and nothing more.

When the doorbell rang, Ava rushed to the door to answer it. The last thing she wanted in the world was for George to receive a tepid response from her mother. She opened the door, and George was there, holding a bottle of wine.

Ava embraced him and George leaned in, giving a polite kiss on the cheek. This told Ava he was interested in her but respected her boundaries, especially since the family was in the other room. They both wore big grins as they walked into the kitchen.

"This is nice," George said as he surveyed the room. "Nothing like my flat with its one bedroom and can't-swing-a-cat kitchen."

Ava laughed. "But it's yours. I'm sharing the house after years of living on my own. No matter your space, it still feels cramped here."

George set the bottle of wine on the counter. "So, what's for dinner?"

Ava had gone all out with a salad and a complicated pasta recipe. She had often used it to entertain her friends in London, and it seemed appropriate now.

"Do you have a corkscrew?" he asked. "It could use time to breathe."

Ava pulled one from the drawer and handed it to him. She watched him as he worked, unable to ignore the rounded biceps that flexed as he pulled out the cork. She hadn't been able to see much of his upper body at the bar, but through the white shirt, she could see a chest that obviously had been molded by exercise.

George caught her spying on him and smiled. He placed the wine bottle again and walked over to where Ava was rinsing the pasta.

Before he could speak, Donna had entered the room. "What are you doing here? What have you done with your cup?"

She ignored George as she looked at the table. "You need to put those back on the table now. We've always done things that way. I see no reason to change the way things have been done."

Ava turned with a flushed face. "We have company. This is George."

Donna went on with her tirade. "Why do you have to entertain here? This is not your house, and you didn't ask my permission to have anyone over." She used air quotes around "entertain," implying that far more would go on. "You could go out for a meal." She turned to George. "You've got a job, right? Spend a little of the cash on my daughter."

"Perhaps we should have gone out," Ava said. She turned away from her mother and began to finish up the pasta.

George was silent, but he appeared to be observing the interaction. Had he been diagnosing the situation as Ava and her mother interacted? The thought scared her. Nothing was good about their relationship.

Luke entered at that moment, taking her mind off Donna's behavior. He snatched a glass from the table and filled it to the rim with George's wine. Ava shot him a glance of disapproval. The wine was for dinner and all of them, not so Luke could get drunk and say whatever inappropriate thing popped into his head.

However, he ignored the hint and gulped down the wine. Luke went for a second glass, but Ava moved the bottle before he could reach it. Even so, Luke became more talkative after the glass of wine.

"So, you're George. I saw you that night at the bar. You were with a group of older women. Are you dating any of them? That's where you two met, right?" he said, pointing at Ava.

George nodded. Before he could speak, Donna had gone into another tirade. "You met at a bar. What kind of girl are you? Did you give it away in the car park? When I met your father, we were properly introduced by a friend. He was a proper gentleman—at least back then. What have things come to these days? Drunks and whores, drunks and whores."

George seemed unmoved by the comments and offered to help Ava with the pasta. She was glad for George's reassuring manner during her interactions with her family.

They sat down to eat. Ava carefully poured the wine, giving most of what was left to the three without a glass. Luke's glass was only half-full.

Ava and George talked about his work, his time in other parts of Britain, and the holidays he'd taken. He seemed very well-traveled for a man who had started in Devon.

"I wish I could travel like that," Ava said. "I've been to France and Spain, but that's it."

George also told her a few charming stories of his adventures in Norway and Poland. For the moment, her mother and Luke were quiet. She hoped the situation would stay that way for the rest of the evening.

When the meal was over, Ava set the plates carefully in the sink, telling her mother she would clean up later. Ava and George had decided to go outside, and George stepped outside. Before Ava could follow up, Donna stopped her and leaned in.

"You need to tell George that your brother is going around the twist, then Luke would understand things better," Donna said.

Ava shook her head. "I'm not saying that." She walked away and joined George outside so they could talk without the family's behavior.

The evening was cool, and they sat on the swing in the back garden, away from the neighbours and street noise. George gave her a big smile and leaned over for a kiss.

Ava felt the electricity between them. Even the night with her family had not ruined their chemistry. He pulled her closer, and Ava opened her lips slightly to let his tongue in her mouth. How long had it been since she'd been enamored with a man?

"That's quite an interesting family," George said, "but I'm sure you know that."

Ava rolled her eyes. "It wasn't easy growing up with all the drama. My mother is not one to keep her thoughts to herself — in case you didn't notice."

Before anything else could happen, she heard someone clearing their throat in the garden. They pulled away and saw Luke standing in front of them. "Sorry to interrupt. I just wanted to know if you had any more of the wine?"

Ava was mortified. Her brother had shattered her private

moment. "No, and I think you've had enough."

"That's easy for you to say, Miss Forgot-Everything. Some of us need a drink to get to sleep every night. Have you had any more since that first one, or was that it?" Luke stumbled off before Ava could speak.

George looked at her. "What was he talking about?"

Ava felt the ambiance change. She cursed Luke and his loudmouth for what had happened. All she had wanted was a pleasant romantic night with this man.

"Luke is having flashbacks. He thinks it indicates that he was abused as a child," Ava said, putting the story into its mildest terms.

"What do you think?" George asked. There was a tone to his voice that Ava was sure he used with his patients. It was calm, yet expecting an answer. Part of Ava resented the professional tone on a date that she'd hoped would be more personal. She had not set up the evening so that she could be analysed. Nothing would make her more uncomfortable.

"I think that he was abused. I don't know what he sees in the flashbacks, but they're rather fuzzy. He's not sure of the where, the when, or who. Just that it happened to him."

"That's not uncommon. The mind doesn't want you to know something this painful. So, the brain tries to provide you with some peace by blocking those memories. That might be what Luke was going through."

"Do you believe him?" Ava asked. She was still trying to deal with Luke's flashbacks and accusations. Yet, George had decided to believe him within seconds of hearing the stories. "He said that he's been having these flashbacks for twenty years, since secondary school."

"That's a lot of weight to be carrying by himself. He still has them?" George asked. "A good therapist could help him work past this and move into a healthier state of mind. I could give him a few names if he wanted."

Ava looked at him. "Please promise you won't take him on. My family is bad enough at present. I would be mortified if you heard all their behaviors."

"No, a good therapist isn't someone who knows the patient beforehand. That's frowned upon. But I have some names of excellent therapists who could help him."

"And you believe what Luke said?" Ava asked. She still wasn't sure what to think. This was all new to her. If it hadn't been for the suicide attempt, she wondered if Luke would have shared any of these details — and would she have begun to have flashbacks as well?

"Only a minor fraction of abuse stories are false. Most of them are accurate. It's best to believe them until you hear otherwise. Are there any other symptoms that might be indicative of abuse?"

Ava told George about what she'd seen at the pub and what Luke had told her. She skipped the part about selling himself for extra cash. There was no reason to share all of their dirty details.

"That's also another sign," George replied. "There's a lack of self-worth, so people do things they wouldn't do. You said he was intelligent and a good student earlier in his childhood?"

Ava had been embarrassed to tell him about Luke, but George took it all in stride. She wasn't keen on how he'd started discussing the situation in a rather clinical, doctorly way. Rather than discussing an awkward family situation, George sounded like he was teaching her.

"I hate to ask," George said, "but what about you? Are you having flashbacks, too?"

"Not like him. If I understand him, he has been having these for years."

"But you have been lately? Like maybe after your

grandfather's death? Traumatic events can bring out memories of abuse, too. Your brain is stressed because of the funeral and staying here, and the memories start seeping out into your conscious."

Ava nodded. She felt like weeping, in part because she had no desire to delve into these dreams and because she felt as though she'd lost George. The electricity they had shared would be lost as they discussed neuroses and other mental issues.

"What are they like?"

Ava took a deep breath. "They're a lot like Luke's own. I see people there with no faces, just hands and touching. I don't know who else was there—if other adults or children were present. I don't know where this takes place. I can specifically see parts of the wall and the staircase, but I don't recall ever being in this place as an adult. And I can't see myself, obviously, so I can't place a date for when it happened either. Luke had more details, but he didn't talk about them."

"In your opinion, do you think that you've been abused — either emotionally or physically?"

Ava thought for a second, but the situation's reality ached inside her. She didn't want it to be true. She wanted things to go back to the other day when she'd been on top of the world, selling a house and being recognised. "I hope not, but it must be true when I think about it. It's so close to what Luke has said."

"So, what do you think about these flashbacks." George took her hand in his, but she felt the pity oozing from him to her. She missed the sparks.

"They only happen when I'm about to go to sleep. I'm not sure if they're real or not. They could be bad dreams brought on by Luke's memories. For example, when you have a bad dream after watching a slasher movie. Remember, I didn't start having these whatever-you-call-them until after Luke started talking to me about them."

George smiled. "You think it's more slasher film than real happenings?"

"I don't know. I try to ignore these flashbacks as much as possible. They're getting in the way of everything I need to do before I go back to London."

George seemed more distant after that sentence. Ava wasn't sure if it was because she would return to London and her life there, and he would be trapped in York. She could not see herself returning to this city with its memories and her mother here.

"I don't think they will go away that easily." George still seemed more serious than before. The sparkle in his eye had dissipated.

"I hope they do. I'll do my utmost." Ava wished Luke hadn't polished off the wine. She could use some at this point.

"Why are you so dead set against this?" George asked. His tone sounded frustrated.

Ava started to cry. "I didn't want to talk about this. It hurts. If you want to know why I don't want this to be true—what if, what if it turns out to be true."

"Then you can get therapy and deal with some of the issues. I could recommend someone."

"It wouldn't be you?" Ava said, still sniffling. "I don't want to mess this up."

"No, then I wouldn't be able to see you, and yes, I want to keep seeing you—if that's okay with you."

Ava took a deep breath, trying to get rid of the tears. "Luke's flashbacks are of him at a younger age. If that's true, then my parents had to know about it. You just don't let six or ten-year-olds go out alone to another house. So, the abuser is someone you know, know well enough that your parents would allow you to be with them. I don't want to think it's my dad or grandfather. Can you imagine?"

George pulled her closer, but Ava didn't feel the same pull as earlier. It felt more like he was comforting someone who had something terrible happen to her. "It happens more than you think."

"I haven't been around my family much. My grandfather is dead. My dad is gone, and my mother is not easy to be around. Luke hasn't been easy to talk to. He's in his own world.

But they're here, you know? If something horrible happened, I think I could count on them. If this is true, I'd lose all my trust. It would be scary to be that alone."

Ava dabbed at her eyes. "I don't want to think about this right now. I really wanted to talk about you and me, not traumas from my early life."

"That's fine. I'm never going to press you to go further than you want. That's wrong, and I respect you too much to push you."

Ava nodded. It was good to hear they could discuss difficult situations without splitting up. So many of her dates expected her to nod and agree with everything they said. She wasn't allowed to have her own opinions with them. This felt different.

Even so, she still felt that George was letting his job get in the way of the date. He had heard Luke's comments about the flashbacks, and now he had to run to her rescue because he worried about her mental health. She'd been fine before she got here. Why was this family always so tricky?

"Let's talk about something else," George said. "I won't discuss this again unless you bring it up, fair?"

Ava nodded. "That sounds good to me. There might be a time when I need to talk to you about these flashbacks, but right now, I'd rather talk to you as a possible relationship."

He raised an eyebrow. "Only a possible? Well, we'll have to try and change that."

Chapter 10

Ava, Luke, and George sat in the back garden of Arthur Farley's house. They hadn't wanted to meet at Donna's house. She was too likely to eavesdrop. Ava didn't want to think about how the woman would react if she found out that they had been abused.

It went without saying that she would blame her children for the abuse. Donna never took responsibility for her own mistakes. Someone else was at fault. Then she would tell her sister Vicki, who would tell the entire town of York in under an hour. That was the way she was. Bad news for others was good gossip for her.

George had given them the diaries, which were stashed in the rear of the garden shed. One board of the shed pulled up, and the diaries could easily be pushed into the space. The board fit tight, so they'd never see the hiding place unless someone was looking for them.

For lack of a better word, George had purchased each of them a dream journal. They were so that they could record any memories or flashbacks of the abuse or the things concerned with the abuse.

Ava felt awkward in the discussion group. Since the night she'd told George about the flashbacks and her concerns about the family, she had not had a single vision of what had happened. She wondered if the flashbacks had been a fluke or a sympathetic reaction to Luke's own memories. His diary was filling up with his visions of what had happened, and every time they met, he had more puzzle pieces to bring to the discussion.

Ava wondered if he would ever get to a point where he would recognise the other children, the place where the abuse happened, and who had taken him to that place. Would he get enough to avenge himself by reporting it to the police or the newspapers and bringing all of these people to justice?

Today, he had recalled more details about the cellar where the abuse took place. Luke and Ava had gone downstairs at Donna's house to see if the description matched. However, the recollections did not match up—as they knew they didn't. Before the discussion today, all three of them had gone downstairs. But again, the cellar space didn't match the siblings' memories.

While George tried to minimise his psychology in their presence, he was scribbling away as Luke talked about the differences between the cellars they had visited and the one in their flashbacks.

"We have a set of steps that both of you described as painted white with chipping. The walls are the same, painted white, but not in good shape. The floor is cement with no tile or carpeting. It's not going to be easy to find this. From your description, so much of this could be masked with paint and vinyl. You might not be able to recognise a redecorated space."

Luke got up and walked away. Ava knew he wasn't angry. He was frustrated with the process and the truth. They might never get past this point, knowing that someone had committed the most heinous acts on them, and they would get to go free.

Ava looked around the garden and felt stressed. The home had once been a showplace with plants and shrubbery throughout. Now, the most prevalent plants were weeds.

Luke came back and sat down. He saw Ava staring at the garden and said, "It's a shame. I offered to help with the house occasionally, but the old man wouldn't hear of it. I found a few gardeners who offered to take over, but he refused. He said he didn't have the money for it. That's a laugh. He had more than enough money to hire a full staff for this place for as long as he wanted. He had more money than any of us knew."

"He did?" Ava asked. She, too, had thought her grandfather was skint. He had always made out that he could barely afford to keep the house, but it was not in good repair. Over the years, the occasional birthday and holiday gifts had dwindled to nothing.

"Sure," Luke said. "I was sitting in his room with him one day. This was when he could barely get out of bed by himself, vomiting and shaking. He needed someone to make sure he didn't fall and break something. His bank statement was on the bedside table, and it was open. Can't blame a guy for reading it. He had plenty of money in a current account. Hundreds of thousands of pounds."

"Did you ask him anything about it?" Ava asked. "Find out more?"

Luke laughed. "Not a chance. He'd accuse me of spying on him and only wanting his money. I can hear him now, carrying on. He was paranoid about money. He might have cut me out of his will."

"I thought he didn't have a will," Ava asked, remembering what her mother had said. Donna had said the money was all hers.

"He did at some point. I don't know what happened. He might have destroyed it, or he might have written a new one. I'm assuming that mum told you it's all hers?"

Ava nodded. "That's what she told me."

"Me, too, but you can never tell. The old man was so picky about things. If it hadn't cost him money, I bet he would have changed his will three times a week."

Ava sat and wondered what else had been lies. There was

a weird world of false stories and misunderstandings, and she could barely follow the path to the truth. "Well, at least the home will get a makeover before it goes on the market."

Luke snorted. "It's not going on the market. Mum and Vicki are taking it over. They have plans."

"What do you mean?" Ava said. She had helped Donna with the paperwork for the house. She had thought that the documents indicated the house would be sold. Donna had always been money-hungry; perhaps Ava had just assumed she would want the cash, not the house. It made no sense that Donna would keep the home unless she had plans to make money with it.

"They're making plans. I heard them talk the other day. Come on. I'll show you." Luke stood up and walked toward the house. Ava and George followed him, curious about what was in the house.

They took the stairs up to the first floor. All six bedrooms were on the right and left down the hallway. Ava frowned again, wondering what her mother would do with such a grand house.

Luke opened the first door and pointed to a painted place on the wall that didn't match the original paint. He repeated this with each bedroom. Someone had been in the house, painting a swatch of paint on the wall, presumably to redecorate the home.

Ava thought of George's comments that paint and flooring could go a long way in changing the tone and recall of a particular place. If Donna got her hands on this house, it would look nothing like it had before. Their memories would not match the new paint and updated fixtures.

"That's not exactly proof that she's going to live here. Former owners do this all the time. They stage a house to make a quick sale." Wistfully, Ava thought of her job and missed it terribly. She thought, as she often had over the past few days, that she'd made a mistake about staying in York for a while. George was the bright spot of the time here. The rest was learning about the abuse and dealing with her family's behavior.

Luke frowned at her. "If you must know, Mum told me she'd be moving soon, and I need a place to live. I thought the old man would have left me something after all I did for him here, but he didn't."

"She's throwing you out?" Ava said with some incredulity. Luke had always been Donna's favorite, and cutting the relationship this way seemed unlike her.

"Not throwing me out. Selling the family house and moving into this one."

Ava thought about Luke's statement. She could see Donna wanting to live in a manor rather than her home. She would love to laud her new-found wealth to all of York. But there were also too many questions that Luke wasn't seeing.

Why the rush? Why the secrecy? If their grandfather had not left a will, Vicki and Donna were the heirs. There were no other siblings, and Arthur had never been married. They could take the money and the home at their leisure.

Donna's behavior puzzled Ava. Donna had always kept Luke close at hand. In that way, she could control him and make him do what she wanted when she wanted it. And he would jump to her commands. Luke wouldn't need to do as she pleased if he was on his own. That seemed unlike her mother.

Ava thought Donna could just be trying to outwit her sister and somehow get the upper hand with Vicki. After all, Ava had not seen Vicki's signature on any of the documents she helped her mother with. Donna had expressed a strong desire to forge her sister's name. That could be explained by Donna pulling a fast one on her sister. The faster the will was processed and went through probate the faster Donna could call this her property—along with the money for upkeep.

"Has she talked to a solicitor about the estate?" Ava asked her brother when she came out of her thoughts.

"Yeah, he's a dodgy one too. Not the person I'd use for probate. A mate used him, and the guy doubled his rate—even after they'd signed the contracts. No way, I'd use him, but Mum wouldn't hear of it. She wanted him."

That made sense to Ava. She would not use a reputable solicitor if she were doing something shady.

"Something is going on there," Ava said to George, who hadn't spoken much during their discussion.

"I don't know why you say that. You act like Mum is trying to pull something over," Luke said with almost a whine. "She's not like that. I'm sure she was just saving Vicki the trouble of signing all the papers."

"You know her, Luke. You know what she can be like."

"You've always hated her," Luke said.

Before Ava could reply, Luke stormed out of the house and back down to the road. Ava watched from a window as he took the path back to Donna's current home.

"What was that all about?" Ava asked.

"Luke has a lot of emotions going on. I imagine he's got the same questions you have about who was behind the abuse. He wants to think it was an outsider, but it's just questions. If you bring up your mother's flaws, then he will have to confront the possibility that she was involved in the abuse. How else could a child leave their parents for hours at a time unless the mother or father or both were aware of what was happening?"

Ava nodded her head. She knew the feelings of uncertainty that she had right now. "But why protect Donna so much? She might be the one responsible for all that. My father left when we were young. It's less likely that he took us to those people."

George shrugged. "He's not my patient, so I can't determine what's going on—and if he was my patient, I couldn't tell you anyway. If I had to guess, I'd say he's struggling to support her. She is throwing him out. She's doing something shady with the solicitor, and he wants to believe that Donna still loves him deep down. Your mum is not an easy person to live with."

"You got a degree to tell me that?" Ava asked. "Ten minutes, and I could have told you that."

"Let me run something by you," George said, clearing his throat and looking away.

Ava paused and wondered what he was going to tell her. She dreaded the idea that George had been analysing her the entire time they'd been together, and he didn't feel the way Ava did about him and the relationship. She took a deep breath and girded herself for the news.

"You had mentioned having these anxiety attacks and other symptoms since you've been back, right?"

Ava nodded. She was now worried that George would dump her for not being "normal." Previous men had done the same. Even though he had assured Ava that he was not doing any such thing, she continued to fret over any comments he made about the family.

"In my experience, those are not the typical signs of an anxiety attack. Vomiting is usually not related to this matter."

Ava sat up straight. "I've always had these issues since I was a child. The doctor said that it was nerves and that I got these symptoms while I was tense—nervous."

George didn't speak for a moment. He paused and looked out at the weedy lawn. "This was when you were a child? So, your parents took you to the doctor. They selected the doctor. Have you gone to a doctor about it since you've been an adult—when you chose the doctor?"

"The symptoms stopped when you left home?" George said. He let the words hang, and Ava slowly began to understand their meaning.

"You think that my family was making me sick—on purpose?"

"It was just a suggestion," he said.

Ava was glad that Luke had left. It would be too embarrassing for him to hear this. Even if she hadn't seen him in years, she still wanted him to accept her – respect her for what she's done. The worst thing that could happen would be that she'd be seen as a conspiracy theorist who suspected her mother of dumping poison in her food.

"I had thought that maybe I was allergic to something in the house or the food. The food here is different than it is in London. There, I can get anything I want. Unlike York, where fish, chips, and beer are staples."

"You had thought of this?" George said. "You entertained the idea that your meals were making you sick?"

Ava sighed. "Not in that manner. I thought maybe something I ate made me sick. Not that my mother was trying to kill me."

George smiled. "It's not as dire as the Borgias. If she really wanted to kill you, she'd dump a bottle of the stuff into your food. You'd have been dead years ago. It's not a matter of killing you for any reason. Maybe I'm wrong, but I'm just worried about you staying in that house. It could be dangerous."

Ava was far too upset to go home now. She had images in her head of poison and death. She hated to think that Donna was hurting her in any way, but the recent flashbacks had made it impossible to keep that ideal. Her family had actively abused her or turned a blind eye to the situation. Now George suggested that Donna had poisoned her, making her ill, but for what reason? She felt that everyone was against her, and she had to have some sense of control.

Ava made her excuses to George and decided to head to the Solicitors her Grandfather used to use, since it was only down the road and could possibly give her the answers she needed.

She walked into the musty office. Mr. Watkins was sitting at his desk. The man looked the same as he had for decades, not aging at all. His hair was still dark brown with a touch of grey on the sides. He had wrinkles around his eyes and mouth, which were not deep or overly noticeable. Ava wished she knew his secret.

He stood up when he saw her. "Why Miss Ava! I haven't seen you in ages. I'm so sorry to hear about your grandfather. I can't believe he's gone. He was one of those people who made you believe they'd be around forever." He was still thin, and his suit hung off him like a tent. Perhaps she had not remembered him correctly? Why was memory such a strange function of the brain?

Ava thanked him. Right now, she was not in the mood to revel in her family's attributes. Once again, she wished she was in London.

"What can I do for you? I'm sure you didn't come here just to visit an old man."

Ava decided to be subtle about this since she knew Mr. Watkins would likely tell her mother about the visit. "Years ago, there was a painting that I loved in my grandfather's house. He promised to leave it to me in his will. I don't think it's worth much—I mean, I could buy my own if I wanted to. But I wanted it for the memories more than anything. Could you check and see if he did that?" Ava dabbed at her dry eyes, hoping for a good performance.

Ava could tell from the man's surprise and the struggle to

get his emotions back under control that she might have hit a nerve. "My dear, I'm so sorry. He didn't leave a will. He talked to me many times about doing it—like so many people do- yet we at the law firm never saw it. At one point, he commented about a will, as though the document was done, but when we asked him to bring a copy in for us, he demurred. I'm so sorry."

She nodded. While she was here, Ava decided to try another trail with him. "I was wondering, too. If the estate would include something for my father, how could he be reached if there was a bequest for him?"

Mr. Watkins's eyes widened. "Well, I don't know. Your mother never said anything about a divorce, but she wouldn't. I was her father's solicitor. It would be odd if she had. But I assume she got a divorce, so your father would get none of it. However, if she had not divorced him, then yes, I am afraid that he might get half of the estate, and yes, in that case, we might have to locate your father. I personally have not seen him since he left town. But to answer your question, I don't know where he currently is. If he didn't come forward, we would need to use a detective to find him. We've done that before, but it's quite awkward. Sometimes they come back and want everything they're entitled to, and in other cases, they want nothing to do with the past."

Ava tried her best to look disappointed, which was simple given that she was upset that she hadn't learned anything new. She honestly couldn't imagine Mr. Watkins lying to her. If there was no will, why was her mother hurrying to push the house transfer? Donna always had an ulterior motive; in this case, she must have a reason for the rush. It would not surprise Ava to learn that her mother knew exactly where her father had been all these years and simply held the knowledge from them.

Mr. Watkins escorted Ava to the door and wished her family well. She left the office feeling more confused than ever.

Chapter 11

Ava heard a knock at the door. At 3:45 a.m., she glanced at her phone. She rolled over and tried to ignore the sound. However, the sound came again—and then again. She finally got up and unlocked the door.

George's questions about her health and the anxiety attacks had made her start locking her door. Ava felt so uncomfortable that she had eaten out twice this week. Fish and chips were getting to be a bit much.

She opened the door and saw Luke in a nervous state. "It's almost four."

Luke pushed his way into the room. His hair was disheveled as if he'd been sleeping. He wore a T-shirt and jeans, and his feet were bare. "We have to talk," Luke said in a soft but urgent whisper.

"Not now," Ava said, flopping back on the bed. She closed her eyes, but he didn't take the hint. She hadn't been sleeping well, and more discussion of their flashbacks would only make it worse.

"We need to talk about this. I saw more tonight. I saw some things that might help us learn more about what really happened." Luke's eyes were wide, and Ava wondered if he'd been taking some sort of drug. He seemed manic, frenzied about what was going on. She couldn't imagine being this upset about a situation that had been replayed in his mind for two decades.

For the past week or so, Luke had been having dreams, more like nightmares, where he would see flashbacks of the abuse itself, not the place or the people who had tortured them, but the actual acts of abuse. Each detail was verified by the two siblings. In one, he'd seen a t-shirt that Ava recalled. In another, she had a bracelet she'd received in primary school. Each of the pieces of the puzzle fit. They had been young, no more than ten by Ava's guess, and more than one adult was involved.

Each of the details had been accurate. Ava had been skeptical with the first few, but as they added up, she became more accepting of the facts. She'd been abused by people that neither of them could recollect.

She opened her eyes and sat up. "What did you see tonight?"

Luke shook his head. "It wasn't what I saw."

Ava put her head in her hands. "Now's not the time for puzzles and guesswork. What did you see?" This was going to be a long night.

Luke said, "It wasn't what I saw, but what I smelled."

As Luke explained to her, he had been in the same cellar as before. The same cruel acts played out in his mind. Even though he'd wanted to wake and avoid the pain of these flashbacks, he hadn't been able to rouse himself. He'd been forced to watch it, similar to how he'd been forced to see those crimes from decades earlier.

As he began to see the same acts being committed on him, the touching he didn't want, he began to experience other senses, not just sight and hearing.

He could smell the damp cellar as well. He could describe the various smells of the stench of sweat and other bodily fluids during one of those abusive sessions. Now, he knew even more.

"And it smelled like lager," Luke said.

Ava squinted her eyes at him. "That's pretty specific." She wasn't sure that she could tell a lager from a stout.

Luke shrugged. "Spend a lot of time in the pubs, you

know?"

"So, you smelled a pint or two," Ava said. "What does that mean?"

"The cellar must be below a pub, restaurant, or place serving alcohol. The smell was too vibrant. It wasn't just a vague scent; it was overpowering."

"And you're sure of this?" Ava asked. She didn't want to sound skeptical of the things he saw. Luke had many more flashbacks than Ava did. He saw things and experienced more than she did.

"It's weird, but I do. I can't explain why I know." Luke's voice cracked, and Ava wondered if he would begin to cry again. Over the past few nights, he'd shed more than a few tears trying to tell Ava what he'd seen. This experiment wasn't good for him.

In her way, Ava was glad that she hadn't witnessed these flashbacks. His were so gruesome and vivid that they made her sick. If her mind were holding back on allowing her to relive that time in her life, she would not complain. She feared what she might learn while staying here.

Luke gazed down at her, studying her intently. "What about your flashbacks?" he asked.

This point had been a problem between them for over a week now. His flashbacks were intense. He woke up sweating and nauseous. Those events made Ava think of George's words about her situation. If Luke was getting sick too after the visions, wouldn't that show that one of the symptoms of this stress could be nausea? She bit her lip, trying not to tell Luke what George had told her.

"Nothing lately," Ava said honestly. She slept soundly and woke in the morning without remembering her past. She felt terrible because her own dream journal was empty, barren of any idea of what had happened to her as a child.

Luke scowled at her and nodded. He left the room and closed the door behind him. Ava got up and locked it as well. Her nerves were shot. The number of balls in the air, all juggled by her mother, was more than she could take.

Ava slid into her bed, pulling the covers up her throat. She pushed her thoughts and feelings into the back of her mind and tried to let herself drop off to sleep. She felt her eyelids flutter, and then she was back at another time.

The same images she'd seen before were playing in her mind. She gasped as she looked around the cellar. Luke had been right. The boxes in the corner had words written on them. She couldn't read the words. Was she too young to read in this vision? She hated the thought of being subjected to abuse during primary school. Like Luke, this flashback didn't stop, although she willed it to an end. She saw bottles and pictures of various types of alcohol printed in black on the boxes. Luke had to be correct. This cellar belonged to some business that served alcohol. There was no way that a family or families could go through this much booze in a year. She looked around for other signs of where she was, but nothing came to mind.

Then, a voice came out in the flashback. "You always come out smelling of roses." Ava didn't have to process who was speaking. It was a catchphrase that Donna always used in the contempt of her daughter. Whenever Ava did well in school, excelled in sports, or caught a boy's eye, Donna lashed out, and she had used that sentence to put her in her place. Ava had forgotten the cruel ways in which Donna had made Ava feel small. Now, the voice and the saying came back to her. She could remember all the nasty things that her mother had spewed.

When she left for London, her mother had used that sentence against her daughter. She told Ava that she would end up on the street, selling herself, because Ava wouldn't be good enough to make it to London. Her mother had laughed at her aspirations.

Her present-day mind asked her repeatedly as the scene played on in a loop, was George right?

When she woke at 8 am, Ava didn't want to get out of bed. She dreaded the thought of seeing Luke and her mother. Luke would want to know more about the flashback. Honestly, she couldn't tell him if the vision was correct—or if she had just heard his own memory and she had added it to her own memories. How could she know what was hers and what was his?

As for seeing Donna, Ava wasn't sure she ever wanted to see her mother ever again. That flood of harsh memories of her mother beating down her hopes and dreams was more than she could handle. And if Ava showed any sign of sorrow or weakness, she knew that Donna would attack her again.

Finally, she got up, knowing that they would come to check on her soon. Luke was downstairs eating a banana. He looked up, and his eyes widened as he saw her. "You saw them. Right?"

Ava nodded, not wanting to say more. The whole experience had exhausted her. She didn't want to think about it and felt sick to her stomach. She thought of George's accusations last night. Nothing had made her ill last night—except the past.

Chapter 12

Donna whistled as she slid by Ava in the kitchen. The space was adequate for one cook. However, when Ava had announced that George would be coming over for a special evening tomorrow, Donna had offered to take Luke out for dinner so they could be alone. Ava had expected her mother to call her names and hint at sexual liaisons between the pair.

Instead, she had been kind and offered to make dinner for the family while Ava practiced her long-forgotten skills in the kitchen. Most things in London were eaten out or ordered in. Cooking dinner for two was stressful enough and this was only the second time George would try her food.

Donna looked over her daughter's shoulder and said, "What exactly are you making love?" The question and its terms of endearment shocked Ava. She wasn't used to kind words, especially when they would be appreciated.

Luke came down and flopped down in a chair at the table. "Two dinners? That's my type of meal," he said, trying to smile. Ava saw the deep lines around his eyes and the bags underneath them. Luke was obviously not sleeping well, and it would only be a matter of time before Donna noticed and demanded to know what was going on.

It was all as though the siblings only had a minimal amount of time before their secret investigation blew up in everyone's faces. Donna had an unexplainable instinct when it came to the things going on around her. Ava was surprised that the woman hadn't pounced on the flashbacks and abuse yet.

Donna squeezed by her daughter and smacked Luke on the

shoulder. "Get up and help. Your sister is busy, and I'm cooking. That leaves you."

Luke reluctantly got up from the table and began setting the places. Ava nearly cringed when she saw the blue ceramic mug come out again. She despised that memento of her youth, especially now that her younger days were tarnished by the flashbacks and returning memories.

Ava paused for a second and thought about her father. Had he known of the abuse? Was he involved in it? Perhaps he had run away, not because of her mother's behavior, but because he knew what was happening here. Ava had always idolised the man and couldn't believe that he'd abused either one of his children, but she could make a case for that conclusion.

She paused in front of the stove, thinking.

"Your stir-fry is burning," her mother said. "It's going to be as black as your soul." Donna laughed at the comment, another phrase she'd used since they were kids.

Ava looked, and the heat on her cooker had been turned up. Instead of level four, the heat was set for level nine, a sure bet to burn the food in minutes. Though she hadn't been paying attention, Ava suspected her mother had done this to undermine Ava's confidence for tomorrow night. It was just like her mother to do something like this.

Ava pulled the saucepan off the cooker and set it aside. The family had no wok, so other means were needed here. Maybe her grandfather's home had a wok, or Donna could buy one with the money Luke had told her would be inherited.

Ava took a spoon and scraped a small amount of the food out of the pan. The food was not bad, as long as she didn't daydream about tomorrow. Ava hoped that George would be giving her other things to contemplate.

Donna sat her meal on the table and urged Ava to leave her practice dinner for later. "You can try again later if you want.

We have the ingredients."

Ava internally debated getting a wok tomorrow for the dinner. She wanted everything perfect even if she knew George wouldn't care about such details. He seemed to care about her, and that warmed her heart.

"Come on now," Donna said. "We're going to be done, and you won't have started yet."

Indeed, Luke was wolfing his dinner down as though he hadn't eaten in weeks. He tried to say something, but a few particles flew from his mouth. He turned his attention to the plate and ignored what had happened.

He took a drink from his ceramic cup, and Ava noticed that he didn't seem to have the same disdain for the cup from their youth. Maybe he didn't associate the two, but Ava found it hard to put it to her mouth, knowing now what had happened decades before.

She tried a small sample of the dinner, and the roast and gravy were delicious. Ava assumed that Donna had dipped into her father's estate to pay for a meal like this. She was used to hot dogs and Ramen noodles. "This is great," Ava said, facing her mother.

Donna beamed. "Eat up. There's more here if you'd like." Donna put some more on Ava's plate. Donna sat down and began eating. Putting herself last was not the norm for her mother. Ava wondered what was going on with her.

Luke grabbed some more of the potatoes and smiled as he ate.

Ava finished the plate and stopped eating. She didn't want to eat too much right now. She took another sip from her cup and put it down. Ava hoped that this new appetite indicated that Luke was improving and feeling more like himself.

"Do you want any more?" Donna asked. "Otherwise, I'll get rid of it. There's not enough to keep for another day."

Donna cut a small piece of meat for her daughter and a larger piece for Luke. Scraping the plates clean, Donna took them to the sink. Ava noticed that her mother had not eaten much of dinner. It must have cost their family a great deal of money, yet Donna had not finished much.

Ava helped Donna clean up the plates and bowls while Luke sat at the table. She wondered for a second if Luke was having the same types of attacks that she had. However, she didn't want to bring this up before Donna. The shit would hit the fan if Donna thought that her two children suspected her of poisoning.

She had wiped off the table and begun to dry some plates her mother had scraped and washed when her stomach began to rumble. The symptoms were like her previous anxiety attacks. The sore throat, the upset stomach, the hot and cold feelings. She thought of all the times she had experienced this in the past. Now was not the time to have another one.

Usually, she could tie the event to a crisis or an argument with her mother, but tonight had been calm and peaceful. What had happened to her? It seemed as if her symptoms were getting worse. Ava worried that she would stop being able to eat meals without a reaction.

"I'll be back in a minute," Ava said, thinking that she had to throw up before the symptoms became worse. She hurried to the upstairs bathroom, forgetting to shut the door as she rushed to the loo. She felt her throat contract, and Ava shoved her finger down as far as it could go. The retching began immediately, coming up in painful heaves.

Though Ava was still looking down, holding her hair out of the way, she heard her mother's voice. "Is this what you do after dinner? I should have known this. No wonder you could stay so slim. You're making yourself throw up. My daughter has bulimia."

Ava tried to ignore her mother, wanting to push her finger down her throat again. However, Donna grabbed her arm.

"Here now, you won't do this in my home. This is a respectable home, and I won't have you throwing up to get rid of a perfectly lovely dinner."

Ava thought that this was so typical of her mother. Ava was sick—painfully ill—and her mother worried about the food and what the neighbours would say.

"Get up now," Donna said. She tugged Ava's arm until she had to stand up. She didn't want any more pain than she had now.

"Are you happy?" Ava said. She knew that trickles of spittle were running down her face. She turned and heaved again, the vomit spilling out of her nose and mouth—this time with more pressure and urgency than the one before. Ava didn't know how much more she could take. The rumbling in her stomach indicated she was far from done with this event.

"You need to go to the hospital," Donna said, pulling out her phone. "My little girl is really sick. It must be that crap that you burned on the stove. Burned food can make you ill."

"My date is tomorrow," Ava said. While she knew that George would want her to seek help, she looked forward to spending time with him—and perhaps moving their relationship to the next level. Instead, she would be a pale, fragile woman with chunks of dinner on her face. She rubbed her arm across her cheeks, worrying what George would think if he was at the hospital when she arrived.

"George will be fine. He's a man. He'll understand that women get sick." Donna shook her head and punched the 999 number on the phone.

"He won't if he knows I'm in the hospital. He'll think I ghosted him." Ava felt the wave of nausea coming upon her again. She wasn't sure how long it would be before she had to throw up again—while her mother berated her.

"Fine. If that's how you're going to be, give me your phone." Donna held out her hand. Ava felt like she had no choice. The sickness was getting worse, and Donna was insistent. Ava was too weak to argue.

Her mother took the phone out of her hand and tucked it away in her jeans pocket.

"He's in my contacts, just the name George," Ava said. She didn't remember hitting the floor or the sounds of the sirens approaching her house.

When Ava awoke, she was alone. Within seconds, Ava recognised the hospital bed where she rested and the IVs running out of her arm. Her mother must have called the 999 exchange after she passed out.

However, no one was there. Her door was open slightly, but she couldn't see anyone in the hallway either. The other bed in the room was empty, and the hospital was relatively quiet.

She wanted to call someone and tell them that she was awake, but Donna must still have her phone. Ava recalled the scenes in the loo just before she passed out. There was no other possibility since she ended up here.

She closed her eyes. Her abdomen was sore, and the never-ending contractions from vomiting had gone on for hours.

When she woke again, the nurse checked her vitals in the room.

"Hello," the nurse said, oozing cheeriness that Ava didn't have. "I'm glad to see you awake."

"What time is it?" Ava asked. The sun was out, but she had no sense of time. Her watch was missing from her wrist, and her phone was still missing.

"Four p.m.," the nurse said before taking Ava's wrist for a pulse check. "You've been out of it a while."

Ava breathed a sigh of relief. At least she could still go

home and make dinner. She hated the thought of missing an evening with George, though Ava was uncertain if she could stand long enough to cook. This anxiety attack had hit her harder than most of the ones she could remember. "I had plans for this afternoon."

The nurse looked at her for a second before talking. "You do know that this is Thursday? You were admitted on Tuesday evening. So, it's been a while. You were sedated to ease the vomiting. You've been out for thirty-six hours."

"Oh," Ava said as the thoughts ran through her head. What had happened to her? Where was George, and what had her mother done with her phone?

The doctor came in as the nurse was leaving. "Hello, I'm glad to see you awake. The nurse indicated that you're awake and alert. Those are excellent signs. Do you recall what happened to you on Tuesday night?" He smiled at her, but the rest of his face did not match that grin. He was hiding something from her, and she wanted to know what.

"I had a family dinner with my brother and mother. I felt ill while I was cleaning up and got sick. I threw up, and then my mother called the emergency number." Ava was surprised that she didn't know more about the evening. It felt like it had been longer, though those memories were gone.

She thought again of the flashbacks she and Luke had experienced. Just like now, her brain seemed to be blocking out what had hurt her. It must be a defense mechanism designed to keep her from feeling the pain of the events.

"You cooked the meal? You cleaned up?" the doctor asked, writing notes as he asked questions. The scratches of pen on paper were the only sound in the room.

"I cooked a practice meal. It was burned. I think my mother turned up the burner. My mother cooked another meal, roast and the helpings. I just helped clean up afterward."

"Did you suggest cleaning up, or did she?" the asked continued.

Ava thought back to the evening. "I think she started cleaning up, and I went to help her."

"Were other people in the room with you and your mother? You said something about a brother. Was there anyone else at this dinner?"

"Luke, my brother, was there. Probably my aunt Vicki was there too. She's there almost daily, but I didn't see her."

"Is that it?"

Ava nodded. She didn't understand why the doctor could care so much about the meal clean-up or the guests.

"Can you tell me about the meal?"

"Couldn't someone else tell you what we ate?" Ava said as the wash of sleep ran through her. She did recall that it was a special meal, perhaps a celebration, though Ava didn't know the source of the festivity.

"I'd rather hear it from you. Witnesses can be unreliable all the time. So, you had what?"

Ava continued the questions for another five minutes before the doctor closed the pages and put his pen in his pocket.

"We'd like to keep you for another day or two. I have concerns about the cause of this illness. The tests won't be painful, and you can go home then if you want." The last words struck Ava. Why would she not want to go home? Did the doctor know something that he wasn't sharing?

Ava was unsure what to do. Her brain was still too foggy to make good decisions, yet she felt alone without good advice. "Is Dr. Shaw here?" Ava asked, hoping to discuss the situation. After all, he'd been the one to warn her about the food and her upset stomach.

"Yes, Dr. Shaw is here, but he's with other patients. We will provide you with a psychologist to talk to, but it won't be Dr.

Shaw. We decided it would be a conflict of interest —given that you two know each other. We try to make sure that our patients get objective help with their issues."

Ava attempted to make sense of all the facts in what the doctor said. George knew she was here. Yet he hadn't come to see her. Didn't he care that she was in the hospital? It didn't make sense. Things seemed to be going so well, and now that she was ill, he'd ghosted her. Did he suspect that she had done this to herself—in the same way that Luke had tried to kill himself with pills? Ava didn't have such medications, but there was likely something in the house with the same effects.

Then, she couldn't figure out why she was being given a therapist to work with. Maybe the doctors had finally listened to her regarding the anxiety attacks and were going to help her cope with them. After all, the spells had spiraled since she'd been here. That only showed that her family was the cause of the stress. It would be nice to deal with them without these attacks.

She leaned back against her pillow and realised the doctor continued talking. "We'll be running some more tests today. We'll know more then, and we can talk." He smiled and then left the room.

Chapter 13

In the morning, Donna brought Ava's phone back to the hospital. She was far more chipper than usual and had plenty of stories to tell her daughter, even though they'd only been apart for three days.

"Did you call George?" Ava asked. "I haven't heard a word from him."

Donna rolled her eyes. "Yes, dear. I called and left a message for him. Men are like that. They're fine with you until something happens, and then you never see them again. Look at your father. I haven't heard a word from him in over twenty years. You'd think he'd want to know how his children turned out, but no, not a word. Get used to it."

Her mother talked about Ava's father for five minutes. She wondered about him. Was he near enough to know that Ava was in the hospital? If he was aware of it, would he come to visit? She doubted it, but Ava still hoped that he would come home to see her.

"Do you know where he is?" Ava asked.

"That piece of work? No, I don't, and why would I?"

"If he left so abruptly, I just wondered how you got a divorce from him."

Donna's face was angry, and her eyes squinted at her daughter. "Well, whatever they're giving you must be powerful. I haven't had to talk about that—man—in ages. When it happened, your grandfather and I—along with his solicitor-- prepared the paperwork for the divorce. I sent it to his mother. She had him sign it and sent it back."

After Donna left, Ava checked her phone to see if her mother had told the truth. In recent calls, she found short messages for George's number. However, there were no messages back to her, and the doctor had indicated that George knew about her illness. Yet, she had still not heard from him.

Ava sat up in the bed. There was no use in fretting. He would call, or he wouldn't. Ava had been through break-ups before, and if he had been like this, she would have been better off without him. The words sounded good, but her heart ached for the man. He had seemed so right for her, but now he wasn't.

Somehow or another, Simon had found out about her illness, and Ava had received flowers from her ex-boyfriend. She wasn't sure how she felt about it, but it did underscore that other people cared more about her than George did.

Ava decided to focus on finding her father and learning more about his role in the will and the estate. One area where her mother had not told the truth was the story about the divorce. Mr. Watkins clearly said he hadn't worked on her parent's divorce, yet Donna had said that her grandfather and the solicitor had worked with her.

She could now see why Donna was in a hurry. The sooner the whole thing was done through the courts, the better. Her father would not hear of the estate, and he would never be able to collect half of Donna's share. Luke had told her that it was sizable, and she believed it.

When the nurse came to release her from the hospital, no one was there for Ava, even though she had texted Luke and George. Neither showed up. She was wheeled down to the doors, where she managed to get a cab home. She felt embarrassed that no one else cared enough to take the time.

When she was dropped off, the house was empty. Ava took the bag of pills and instructions with her and walked up to her old bedroom. The house was empty, and she was alone.

She pulled her phone out of her pocket and saw that George had left a message for her. She opened the app and read the message. She began to cry and then got angry.

George's message had been simple. "I missed you the other night. I came to your house, and no one was there. I didn't find out about your story until a nurse at the hospital told me. I felt humiliated that I had to learn this from another person, not you. I thought we were growing together, but I guess you didn't consider me when you needed someone to help you."

Ava read the note again and then heard the door slam downstairs. She took her phone and marched down the steps to confront her mother.

Donna was putting away food and drinks when Ava came into the kitchen. "You, you did this."

Her mother turned around. There was some emotion in her eyes that Ava couldn't understand. "Dear, are you not feeling well? I don't know what you're talking about."

"George just told me that he didn't get any communication from the family the night I went to the hospital. Nothing. I asked you, and you told me that you had."

"My dear, I did. You can look and see that I called the number you gave me." Donna reached out for the phone, but Ava jerked her arm away so that Donna was no longer in range.

Ava looked at the messages again. There were two calls to George. The first one longer than the second. She puzzled over the message for a second. Tapping the message and the name, the phone number came up for George. But it wasn't his number. She looked again. From what she could tell, a second George Shaw contact had been added to her contact list, and the second one—the one with a different number—had been used to "call" George that night. It had all been a nasty prank played on Ava. It would look like he'd been called when he hadn't, and when he didn't hear from her, it would drive a wedge between the two. Just what Donna had wanted.

Ava wasn't sure why her mother didn't want her to be happy, but that was her motivation. Perhaps Donna didn't want to see her daughter happily in love when her husband left her for unknown reasons. Was Donna jealous of those who could keep a relationship going?

She turned and said to her mother, "I'm going to find my father. I'm going to ask him if he's divorced from you. Mr. Watkins said that he never worked on your divorce. So maybe he's still your husband. And if he is, I will tell him about his inherited fortune."

Donna's response was immediate. She lunged at Ava, practically snarling with anger. "You had better stay out of this. You have no idea what you're getting into, and you'll get hurt if you do. You'll be hurt like you've never been hurt before."

Ava shivered. The threat was there and put into words she'd never heard before. What did her father have on Donna? But now she wanted to know what it was and what he had on her. Something was going on that had brought out this reaction.

She backed away a few steps, but at least Ava had found a trigger for her mother. What did Ava not know about their father?

Going back upstairs, Ava decided to make a plea to George and explain what had happened – her mother's plot to break them up. Ava still wasn't sure of the other woman's motivation. Why would her mother care about Ava's romantic life, given that Ava would be going back to London soon? What did it mean to her?

She pulled out her phone and looked at the fake calls to George again. She could barely see straight. She was that angry. Even though George knew of her issues with her own family, he had bought their tricks and moved away from her.

Ava called. The phone went to voicemail immediately,

likely meaning he'd decided not to communicate with her. Ava left a long message explaining what had happened and how her mother had come between them. She apologised for the situation and asked him to call her back.

Luke knocked on the door after she hung up. Ava wondered how long he'd been standing there and what he'd heard. Ava knew she should have shut and locked the door before calling, but she'd been too upset.

"Hey, what's going on with you and mum?" Luke asked. "I heard some yelling."

Ava suspected that her brother had heard everything and was just asking to see if he could learn more. Donna had not been quiet, and Ava had matched the same sound level.

"She lied to me. She faked the phone calls, so it looked like she had called George for me—to tell him that I was in the hospital. She created a second contact for George to make it look like she'd called him."

"And George didn't take it well?"

"Worse than that. He broke up with me by phone. I tried calling him back and telling him what had happened, but he's not taking my calls." Ava's voice cracked, and she stopped talking for a moment. She didn't want to cry in front of Luke — or any family member.

"Wow, that's bad." Luke didn't look at her. He stood against the door, eyes looking down.

"Has she done that to you?" Ava asked, now wondering if Luke's feelings came from previous experience.

"Yeah, on the few times I've had a real date. Yeah, she has." Luke looked up at her. "I'm not sure why she doesn't want us to get involved. She tells me I wouldn't be good in a marriage — like our father. I don't remember him, so it's not much of an insult."

Ava nodded. "What's going on with our dad and her? I

mentioned that I wanted to find him. She nearly took my head off."

Luke laughed. "I'm surprised you're still here. The last time I mentioned something, I had to go stay with some friends until she calmed down. It was a few days. I think his leaving made a mark on her. She hasn't dated anyone since he left."

Ava thought about her brother's statement. What had happened between their parents to make their mother so hateful to her children? And why had Donna never dated again? It seemed like a deep scar.

Ava would have to ask around and find out what she could about her father. The family was out. She couldn't ask Vicki. She would run back to Donna in a heartbeat to tell her everything. Her grandfather was dead, and her mother was angry.

Luke gave her a small wave and left the room. This time, Ava shut the door and locked it from the inside. She didn't want any interruptions tonight. She only wanted sleep.

Chapter 14

However, sleep did not come that night—or the early morning. Ava had suffered from dreams and flashbacks all night long. She wasn't sure if they were brought on by talking to Luke before bed or if the emotions from the fight with her mother and the breakup with George. Everything felt too much.

She noticed two things as she sat up. The pillow was wet in places where she'd cried through the night. She tried to remember all the flashbacks, but she couldn't. They must have been intense, and once again, perhaps Ava's mind had repressed those memories to keep her away from the pain.

The second was a scrap of paper on the nightstand that read "Queen's Head." She tried to figure out what the words meant, and then she remembered.

In her flashbacks, she recalled being taken to a pub named The Queen's Head. A hand had grabbed her wrist, pulling and tugging her along. Even at her young age—and Ava had not yet determined how young she was—Ava knew that bad things would happen at that pub. She could recall the pub's sign clearly.

Once inside the pub, the hand and Ava had gone to the cellar. She had been partly dragged to the bottom of the stairs. There, she recognised the walls and the marks on the stairs. This was the same place she had seen before. The markings were the same. Even the beer barrels were the same.

Ava had fought some more, but a hand had slapped her across the face. Even in the flashback, she could feel the sting—

the ache of knowing what would happen to her. Other hands grabbed her, and she struggled. However, these were adults, and she was a child. She could hear the other children as they cried and screamed at the abuse.

Ava wished the flashbacks would end. Why was she plagued with them now? What had happened to her life that had opened the door to these memories? Ava wanted to know, but simultaneously, she hesitated to find out. What if the answers were even worse?

She decided to try at least to find the pub where these crimes had occurred. If nothing else, it would provide her with some sense of closure. The pub would allow her to see that these flashbacks were not fake, not a figment of her imagination, but real and true.

Ava thought about this plan for a minute. She was scared to do this for the same reasons. She would have to realise that she had been abused as a child. The pain and the humiliation would be difficult to bear, especially now that she'd be on her own.

After she had eaten a small breakfast, she would discuss the plan with Luke and see if he would help her. She wasn't sure if the vendors and shop owners would help her find the pub, but she was more likely to succeed with a long-time York resident. She would only be called a stranger.

Luke was less enthusiastic than she was. "So, you think you know the name of the pub? I've never heard of it. That doesn't get us too far." He took his phone out of his pocket. It was an earlier model and looked beat up. He typed a few keys and then read the page in silence.

"Did you find something?" Ava asked, kicking herself for not thinking of a Google search first.

"Nope, no such pub in a twenty-mile radius. Do you remember anything else when you were being dragged around? Perhaps like the shop next to the pub? That would give us an idea of the location, even if the pub is gone now."

Ava tried to recall, but the images were too vague to remember the area around the pub. She only saw shadows and the hand that dragged her down the street. Her memories were far from complete.

"Well, what type of hand was it?" Luke asked. "You should be able to tell me that."

Ava thought back to it again. "It might have been a man. I don't know. The fingernails weren't painted, but that doesn't mean anything. They could just have been polish-free."

"Vicki doesn't wear polish," Luke said.

Ava was startled by the comment. Was he thinking that Vicki had been a part of the abuse conspiracy? The mere thought of a family member harming their own family for their pleasure disgusted her. Yet Luke was obviously thinking along those lines.

"So, how do we find out the location of this pub?" Ava asked, changing the subject sharply.

Luke shrugged. He had lost interest in the topic. Ava wondered what had shut him down this way. She focused on the situation rather than determining what was going on in his mind. She had a

"What about the library?" Ava asked, looking for references that might have information about the Queen's Head.

"Why not Google it?" Luke asked. He had his phone out and began typing. He sighed again. "Nothing. I can't find any particular mention of it."

"That's odd," Ava said, thinking about why the pub would be a secret or close to it. Most of the bars around here would have killed for publicity of any kind, but this one had gone dark. "What about the library?" she asked again.

"Do you think that the library is going to have a whole shelf of books on the long-gone pubs of York? I doubt it. Those ladies are not going to be buying books on booze."

Ava sat down and waited for other ideas to come. Now that she had discovered this pub, she needed to find out if the Queen's Head was real. She was stymied how to learn more.

"What about asking pubs in the area? They might know," she suggested.

Luke put his hands over his face. "That would be a lot of work. Do you know how many pubs there are in York? Then we'd have to find bartenders and owners who were old enough to remember a pub from twenty years ago.

"I wish I could think of a way to find it," Ava said.

"Yeah, this is outside my work training," Luke replied.

Ava wasn't sure what Luke's work was, but the sentence made her think. She was in real estate. Pubs—like homes—were sold, and there were records of the sale. She knew the laws of England and York, though it didn't feel anything like London, was part of the U.K. She could find the records if they had existed at some point earlier than twenty years and learn what had happened to the building. Ava knew that old structures were often demolished, but there was a chance that the pub's cellar was still in use, and it might bring back more flashbacks.

She started to leave, but her phone chimed again. Mrs. Horridge had texted her, asking to meet. Ava wasn't sure why this woman wanted to see her so badly, but Ava ignored the message for now. It would have to wait until other matters were settled.

Chapter 15

Ava was back again at the hospital. For some odd reason, she'd received a call from the doctor who had treated her. He wanted another round of blood work and urine before coming to a conclusion on his analysis.

Ava was nervous about the call. She had heard of people getting odd maladies, and now the doctor wanted another round of testing.

She made her way to the hospital's A&E entrance. Ava explained her situation, and the nurse pointed to a bank of empty chairs.

Sitting down, she wondered about her earlier visit. She couldn't help but remember George and how Donna had split them up.

"Ava?" a voice said behind her.

Ava stood, expecting it to be a nurse who would get the requisite work done. However, George was looking at her.

"What are you doing here?" he asked. He looked around, and Ava wondered what he was looking for. Had he met someone else, or was he embarrassed to be with her?

"The doctor wanted me to come in for some more testing."

George bit his lip, but he didn't answer. He just stood there, staring off into space. Ava couldn't tell what he was thinking. Was any part of him still missing her?

"Do you know what's going on?" Ava asked. "I mean, I know you're not supposed to look at other people's records, but maybe he said something to you?"

George shook his head. "I've heard nothing."

Ava felt he was getting ready to leave, so she spoke quickly. "I've had some more flashbacks. These had backgrounds to them. Luke and I are trying to find out where the cellar is located. I have a few ideas on how to find out."

Ava was right about one thing. George was interested in her comments. "You should…"

"I know. I should take this seriously, and I am. I've had several disturbing images in my sleep, and I've written them all down. I'm seeing someone about all of this and looking into what I can corroborate." Ava was impressed with herself as she enumerated the list of actions. She wasn't planning on getting George back. However, she wanted to let him know he'd been important to her progress in this situation.

"Why don't we take this to somewhere more private?" George said.

Ava wasn't sure if he didn't want others to hear about the abuse –or if it was something more personal. Perhaps George had another girlfriend now, and she wouldn't be happy with a tete-a-tete with his ex-girlfriend. Ava didn't care, though. She thought about what the request for more blood tests might mean and the situation with the will and the solicitor.

George went to the front desk, talked to the person there, and then came back. "I told them to page me if you weren't back in time, and I would tell you so you can get those tests." He winced slightly at the last word, and Ava wondered what that meant. She thought that perhaps George had issues that he hadn't discussed with her. He was acting strange.

Ava sat down, and after the waiter took their coffee order, she looked at him. "So, did you want to talk to me about something in particular?"

"I just was pleased with your progress, and I'm happy to talk to you about that if you need someone who listens."

But not date, Ava thought. She was frustrated that George

couldn't recognise the manipulations from her family while she was growing up and their impact on her. He couldn't see that the same types of lies and tricks were still happening. Ava's only successful future would be when she returned to London with her fulfilling job career and none of her family. She wanted to spit all that out—and maybe that's what George expected, but she wouldn't give him the satisfaction. She would behave like an adult, even though she'd had no role models growing up.

"I think something dodgy is going on with my mother and my grandfather's estate," Ava told him about the desire to rush the will and the conflicting statements she'd received from various people about the will and the estate.

"Do you think your father could be involved in this?"

"It's possible. He could be waiting for the right moment to reintroduce himself and collect his part of the estate."

"And how would you feel if he came back?" George asked.

Ava didn't like the therapist-speak he was giving her. "I would deal with that when it happens. Until then, I'm not too worried about it."

"That's a good attitude to take," George replied. He flashed her a smile that reminded her of earlier times, but she tried to push down the emotions. This was not a reunion. It was only a summary of what had happened recently to her. Ava had heard George's professional attitude, which did not indicate any more than a specialist interest.

"Thanks," she replied. She decided to keep her own responses as cool as could be.

George looked at his watch. "I think it's your turn," he said.

Ava smiled and threw a ten-pound note on the table. She would not have George pay for her unsipped coffee. She was on her own, and she would behave like it.

The nurse was waiting for her at the front desk, and Ava

followed her into the lab room, where the usual arrangement of vials and cups was present. She followed the nurse's directions, who provided no reasons for the second round of testing.

"Did the first set get lost?" Ava asked finally, unable to wait any longer.

"Oh no," the nurse said with a big smile. "Sometimes the tests are inconclusive. Other times, the samples are corrupted, and of course, the doctor might want to see a second sample to see if the first one was correct. We get this all the time. It's no need to worry."

Ava disagreed with the nurse. It was quite distressing. The process itself was over quickly and painlessly, but the thoughts of what was happening haunted her. Combined with the flashbacks, she spent too much time with anxiety and sadness. She wanted to get back to the Ava who had arrived in York a few days ago.

She decided that she would have to take charge and find out where her father lived and the location of the missing pub so she could determine if the memories she had of the abuse were real or imaginary.

Chapter 16

Ava had decided to start looking for the pub in the local bars. If anyone knew about the history of the pubs, it would be the bartenders and the owners who had been there for ages. Luke had been against the quest, wanting to look through records and paperwork.

However, Ava had decided that she needed to be out and around people. She missed the interactions she had in real estate, the excited faces of the buyers, the discussions and negotiations with the other agents, and more. This would be the best way to get a similar set of interactions.

Ava went to the first bar, but the bartender was far younger than her. She sighed and went to the next pub. The bartender was older, and she saw him talking to an older man that Ava hoped was the owner. Between the two of them, she hoped that they might know something about the Queen's Head.

She ordered a beer and waited for a chance to talk to them. She had opted for beer, thinking it would take more of them to get her tipsy. She needed her wits about herself to ask those questions.

"New here?" the bartender asked after he'd served two other customers.

"No, I grew up here. I just have been gone a long time. Came back for a funeral." Ava hadn't expected to share that much information with a stranger, but it blurted out with her nervousness.

"Ah, sorry to hear. How long are you in town for?"

Ava started, realising that the man was trying to ask her

out. While Ava supposed that she could have expected this, she didn't.

"Only a day or so. There was a pub around here somewhere; I used to go to it when I was younger. Queen's Head, have you heard of it?"

The man laughed. "You must be a mite older than I took you for. Hey, Jack."

The man who had appeared to be the owner came out from a room behind the bar. She tried to look in the room as he opened the door, but he was too fast for her. "What do you need? I'm busy."

"I thought you'd get a kick. This lady used to drink at the Queen's Head." The bartender tried not to laugh heartily, but a few chuckles escaped. Ava had no idea what had caused this reaction. She was both intrigued and scared.

"You did now? Then how old are you?"

This was the second time she'd heard this from the men. The pub must be older than she and Luke had expected.

"Maybe I made a mistake. I might have gone there when I was younger," Ava replied.

"I'm sure you did. Now piss off. We don't like to talk about the past."

Ava left the beer on the bar and left.

The next three bars had young bartenders who looked not too bright. She went along the busy center, trying to find another pub that might know something.

At the next pub, the bartender was older. The place was empty except for the two of them, So Ava ordered a second beer and waited for him to talk to her.

"You meeting someone here?" the old man said. His voice was raspy, almost as if he had to push the words out.

"No, I'm looking for a particular pub. The Queen's Head. My family used to own the pub," Ava began. She was not going to fall into the same trap of trying to make people think she was older.

"Your family owned the place, did they?"

Ava nodded.

"You're not welcome here," the man said. He took her beer mug, poured out the contents, and walked away.

With nothing else to do there, Ava left. She was shocked by the man's reaction, but she felt more confident that bad things had happened at this pub—and that it was very real. She stepped out onto the curb and abruptly stopped.

Luke and those same two people she'd seen him with the other night were standing at the door of the pub she'd been to before this one. The man handed Luke some cash, and they all entered the bar together.

Ava didn't stick around. She didn't want Luke to see her hunting down this disreputable pub—and she didn't want to see what was going on with the three of them.

Having given up on the pubs, Ava decided to try the land registry records. The change would be easier on her feet—and the employees would likely be less rude to her. Ava sat on the stool in front of a microfiche machine. She hadn't seen one of these in ages, but apparently, York still believed that these were viable.

She started looking at the documents for the sales ten to twenty-five years ago. She was basing that timeframe off the likely time of her abuse and long enough ago that the pub would not be known now.

Ava was also puzzled about what to look for in terms of the buildings. She had first narrowed it down to business buildings, but after looking at nearly one hundred sales, she reduced the search to pubs and other buildings where alcohol was served. Luke had smelled the drinks in a flashback, and she trusted his memories. Even so, she had high hopes that she could find this pub and confirm that the cellar belonged to them.

Now that she had narrowed the buildings to such a small subset, the work went faster. She could examine the building, its area, and the information about its owner and the change of hands.

One thing that she realised early was that the pub had changed names and owners. The previous name, the Queen's Head, would not help her in the search. She spent nearly five hours on the first day of her search. She got nowhere, though the process was quick.

The following day, she had made it to seventeen years ago when she found something. While looking at the outside of the building, she began to get a flashback. Ava was concerned. What if it was a powerful memory while she was in a public building?

She excused herself quickly and headed to the bathroom. Ava went into a cubicle and locked the door. Putting her head in her hands, the memory was so clear and vivid: the hand that pulled her along, the sign outside the pub with the image of royalty. She could see it clearly. This time, she saw a few of the buildings around this pub. The buildings were older and less well-kept, but business was still busy. No one who walked by noticed her emotions and the crying before being taken into the pub.

The scene seemed to disappear for a few seconds. Then she was on the stairs to the pub's cellar. There was more than one child and more than one adult in the space. She cringed, and the scene stopped.

Ava took a few deep breaths, trying to get her nerves under control. No wonder that she had mistaken these events as anxiety attacks. When Ava's breathing was under control, she stepped out of the cubicle and went to the mirror. The mirror was old, and the reflection only appeared in some places, but it worked well enough so that she could fix her make-up. Given that she would be talking to people, she wanted to look nice. No signs of crying or emotions here. She needed to be confident and alert.

Ava went back to continue her search. She looked around for a clerk.

"Excuse me, may I print this off somewhere?" she asked. The clerk was far older than her, perhaps even older than her mother. She was thin and severe. She had dark hair that had clearly been dyed and glasses that looked like they came from the last century. However, she did fit the vibe of the microfiche and the huge machines that read them.

"Yes, it's a pound per page." The woman nodded to the printer in the corner, which appeared to be not much younger than the clerk.

Ava raised an eyebrow and was glad that the document only had three pages. The clerk took the mouse, and with a few deft moves, the printer was whirring. "You can pay on the way out," she said with a weak smile.

Ava took the pages. Despite the printer's age, they were cleanly printed. She tucked them into her bag and went to the door to pay the woman, who seemed to be the only one working today.

Outside, the sun was bright, and Ava squinted as she looked around. A bus was pulling up and Ava checked the number. She'd gotten lucky.

She had left her car at home, thinking that she would spend the day at the public records office. The bus went to a stop near the pub, though she didn't recall ever taking the bus to it when she was young. She tried to think of where she might have gone on this particular bus route, but nothing came to her. The bus pulled up to the stop, and Ava, along with several other people coming home from work, left the bus.

Ava froze as she stood outside the pub. The blood in her veins froze, and she couldn't move. The sign was gone, and the new name was The Prince Gentleman's Club. No matter what it was named, Ava recognised the building.

When she felt like she could move again, Ava headed to the pub. The door was the same as it had been all those years ago. The paint had been reapplied, but the door's ornate carvings remained the same.

She pulled the door open, just like the hand had done in her flashbacks. Now she could answer Luke that the hand was definitely a female hand. The nail polish had been present, but it was only a clear coat. She could see the traces of lotion and could smell the aroma of the lotion. It was so vivid that Ava could probably have picked it out of a line-up.

The pub was busy. Twenty or thirty customers stood at the bar, everyone demanding a drink. At the moment, there was only one bartender, who had paid no attention to her entrance.

Ava walked to the door as if in a trance. She knew the place, and now she knew the way to the cellar. Steeling her spine, she opened the door and looked back to the bartender. He hadn't looked up at her yet.

She slipped through the doorway and carefully closed the door, making sure that she wouldn't get locked in. The stairs creaked, but Ava doubted that the noise would be heard over the patrons. She made her way down the stairs. The flashbacks had been from the middle of the cellar floor, looking back at the stairs, so she was still uncertain whether this was the place or not. She had to be sure, and that meant seeing it from the same perspective as those images.

She got to the bottom of the stairs and moved to the center of the cellar. She was astounded. The stairs were the same, white with places of missing paint. Some of the scuffed places were still visible on the steps.

The shelves around the room were still usable, and she saw the bottles of booze like she had in those dreams. It was everything she'd seen in those nightmares —and they were real. She couldn't explain it any other way. She had seen these before. They had played in her mind recently, and now she'd found the same place in York.

Ava began to have another vivid flashback as she stood there. Now she saw other hands and other children in the room. The children could be seen, and looking around the room, she saw Luke. He was crying as other hands touched him. She could see many other hands here but no faces. Unlike the children, she only saw one part of the human body, the grasping holding hands of the people who wanted to do evil things to them.

Ava threw up. She wiped her lips off with the back of her hand. She threw up again and then twice more. The feeling was so overwhelming and disgusting. How could adults do that to someone so young?

Ava started to wretch again when she heard the door upstairs open.

"Here now, what are you doing down here?"

The man moved down the stairs much faster than she had. He came over to her and then took a few steps back. "There's a loo for that," he said.

"Sorry," Ava said. Her head was spinning, and she still felt sick. The realisation that this was real, the pub, the abuse, the people who had done this to her struck home —hard.

"Want me to call you a taxi?" he asked, putting a hand on her shoulder.

She shook the hand off, even though she knew it was a friendly gesture and not threatening. "Yeah, that would be great." The taste of vomit was still in her mouth.

He helped her up the stairs and sat her on a stool while they waited for the transportation. She dreaded going home and facing the reality of what had happened.

Ava still couldn't get over the magnitude of what had happened. This was not one abuser and one child. She'd seen her brother there and the faces of other injured children. However, it was the adults that upset her most. The crimes had been committed by more than one person. There had been the hands of men and women, young and old.

These crimes had been organised by someone, some evil person, who had found the location, grouped the adults and dragged the children into the lair. Ava still felt sick, but at the same time, she began to feel empowered. Even though this had occurred decades ago, she would find out who had created this nightmare and bring them to justice.

Chapter 17

Donna was nowhere to be seen when Ava came home. She was surprised at her mother's absence, but given their rough relationship lately, she was glad for the peace and quiet. The house was silent, and Ava walked around the kitchen, expecting to hear someone follow her into the rest of the house. She looked for the papers she'd helped her mother with, but Ava found no documentation regarding the house. She wondered if these had been given to a solicitor for processing or if her mother had hidden the papers so Ava would not be able to see what she was doing, which was exactly what was happening.

Ava went upstairs to her room, where she changed clothes and cleaned up her face. She was still pale and tired, but she had some ideas on how to move forward with investigating the abuse.

She relaxed on the bed, fluffing the pillows so that she could think while resting. There were so many paths she could take right now. Part of her wanted to leave this alone, to try to forget what had happened and leave for London immediately. However, she thought of her brother and the other children. She was not alone here in this crime. Others had been harmed, too.

If she was going to continue, she would need to go back to the records and see who owned the pub, the Queen's Head. If the abuse had been conducted there, the owners had to have known what was going on in the cellar. No one could be that oblivious.

She could also try to follow up on the other children in York who had been used in that way. Ava thought about perhaps visiting a support group or similar group that might have people in the same situation as Ava. She liked that idea since she could also use the time to work on her own issues. She knew, simply from memory loss, that she had been impacted by her past. Some time with others like her might help ease her own anxiety.

Ava wondered if Luke was home. He could perhaps fill in some of the blanks in her memories. The flashbacks came and went, with parts of the image blurred out. Luke seemed to be ahead of her in terms of what he saw and what his other senses told him.

Before she could even get up, Luke was knocking at the door. "Ava got a second?" his voice rang.

She got up and crossed the room to the door and opened it. Luke looked different than he had before. His hair was trimmed and cut in a new style. It didn't look cheap, and Ava wondered where her non-working brother had found the funds for some luxury. His clothes were new, too. A button-down long-sleeved shirt in a tan color that highlighted his darker hair, and trousers that fit like they'd been tailored for him.

"What's up?" she asked when she finished her examination of his clothes. "You're looking good today."

He made a hand motion as if to brush the comment away. "Everything okay here?"

"I found the pub," Ava said, feeling proud of her investigation, even if she'd been sick multiple times.

"What pub?" he asked.

Ava was stunned. They'd been discussing this for days, and now he pretended not to know what she was talking about. "The pub where the abuse was?" She heard her voice go up at the end as if she was asking a question about it.

"Oh, the pub you think was behind the abuse," he said. He actually made air quotes around the last word, as if he didn't believe what she was saying. He wasn't even listening to her story before he began to challenge it.

"You've changed your tune?" Ava shot back.

Luke sighed as though he was humoring a child. "Why don't you show me what you have, and then I can see for myself?"

Ava brought out the documents and showed him a picture of the current landscape outside of the building which included the Prince Gentleman's pub sign. She could see in her mind the dread she had felt as a child every time she saw the front of the pub.

She watched Luke's face as he looked at the pub and then at her. "So, doesn't mean a thing to me. I mean, I don't remember ever going to that part of town. None of the buildings are familiar at all to me."

Ava looked at him in disbelief. All this time, they had been pursuing the same goal, finding the location where they'd been abused. Now, suddenly, Luke acted like he'd never heard of any of this.

Her first thought was that Donna had got to him. Even though they'd been quiet and discussed the matter away from her ears, their mother was sneaky. She could easily install microphones so that she could record and listen to everything said in either bedroom. Would her mother have interfered like this? Ava didn't know. Her mother seemed more interested in Grandfather's estate than anything else.

She had felt that she, at least, had Luke on her side, but with this sudden turn of events, she felt alone again. She thought about returning to London and leaving all this behind. She'd certainly been better off without these family secrets.

She needed to decide a next step in dealing with her

brother.

"Did those people pay you off? I saw you with them again the other day." Ava didn't want to sound as though she'd snooped on him, but at the same time, she had seen them give Luke large sums of money—and today, he had a nice haircut and better clothes.

Luke laughed a short bark that didn't sound amused. "You don't get it, do you?"

"So why are you acting like you never heard of this?" Ava said. She could feel her eyes well up. Of all the responses to her discovery, Luke shocked her with this reply. He had pushed her in this direction, and now he had disavowed it.

"Why don't you just go home?" Luke said. "Go home. We were fine without you here, and now you're just dredging up all these memories and all these lies."

Ava pushed him out of the door, slamming the door locked. She'd had enough of family tonight.

The next morning, Ava got up and dressed and went out the door without seeing anyone. She had no desire to spend the morning with Luke, who would question her own flashbacks and deny his. Ava's mind had not slept well last night. She'd had horrid dreams where people questioned everything that she thought she knew, from her parents to her own name. She'd woke several times, fearing that she'd actually screamed because she had shouted so loud in her dreams.

The kitchen was quiet, and she poured a cup of coffee into one of the to-go cups. She couldn't bear drinking from that childish mug that her mother had had made. It was embarrassing at thirty-five to be treated like ten years old. She washed out the cup and put it back on the shelf.

Ava decided to drive today. She didn't know how long she would be at the public records office, but she didn't want the additional worries of interactions with the family.

When she returned to the records office today, she knew what she was looking for. Originally, she thought that Luke would help her investigate who had owned the pub before its current owners. If she could find the names of the owners, she could move on to find who had been behind the abuse ring.

Ava was determined to find out more. The same woman from yesterday was helping customers and brought the records to Ava. "This should cover everything you're looking for," the woman said. Her attitude was one of disdain, as if she knew what had happened at this pub in its earlier years. Was that possible? Ava had assumed that the pub was a secret known only to Luke and Ava, but yesterday's images had included others. How many of those others had shared their experiences? Did the whole city know the secrets of the Queen's Head? Ava couldn't ask others what they knew. It was both intrusive and suggestive.

She started on the records, glad that today's search had been narrowed to a fraction of yesterday's work. Without much effort, she found the information on the original pub. Indeed, the business had been called the Queen's Head from 1900 to about 2005. The company had gone out of business after that, and the new proprietors had submitted permits for the upgrades to the building and had christened it the Prince Gentleman's Bar. Ava had the proof she needed now to move forward.

Ava had one more stop before heading home for the day - the Solicitors.

Mr. Watkins was sitting at his desk when she opened the door to his office. "Do you have a minute?" Ava asked, looking around the empty space. If he was a working solicitor, he certainly wasn't filled with clients. The seats were vacant, and in the afternoon light, she could see that several of the chairs were dusty, as if no one had used them in weeks.

"Certainly, I do –for you," Watkins said. "What can I help you with?"

She handed him the papers she had printed at the public records office. She pointed to the records for the Queen's Head pub. "I am interested in finding out who owned this. From the records, it looks like a business sold it, but I can't find any information on who owned the company."

He cleared his throat. His finger trembled slightly as he pointed at the record on the page. "Well, my dear, I think—if you have this correct—that this is what's called a shell corporation. It's used by people or persons when they don't wish to be known. Typically, they're used by people who are not very nice and don't wish to get caught doing something illegal. Would you think that is the case here?"

Ava debated how much to tell Mr. Watkins as she drove to his office. She didn't trust him at all, and she thought he might be involved in the swindle her mother was now undertaking with the will. However, a clean and ethical solicitor might not know how a shell corporation works. She was certain that Mr. Watkins did.

"Yes, these are not very nice people. They knew my family; from what I understand, they were quite disreputable," Ava replied. "I want to see if they owned the pub."

He cleared his throat again. "Well, this is not my forte. However, I do know a chap in town who might be able to help you. If you'll excuse me a minute, I shall call and ask him."

Ava saw the door leading to a small office that might have once belonged to a secretary. The door was even dustier than the chairs, so Mr. Watkins went into the room and closed the door.

She tried to strain her ears to hear the conversation, but he was too sharp for that. It was behavior like this that made Ava sure that he was less than scrupulous—which is what she needed at the moment.

The solicitor returned with a smile. "He said that he's happy to help. I hope it's okay, but I provided him with your name as well as the name of the pub. He said he could have something for you in a few days. I do hope that's acceptable?"

Ava was uncertain about giving her information to strange solicitors who likely had a reputation. However, she saw that she had few choices here. This wasn't London, where she could find a dozen such solicitors in a moment. "Thank you. I appreciate your help."

"Well, I'm always happy to help, but of course, there is a fee for the job." The solicitor put out a hand as he named a price.

Ava knew the same task would cost twice that in London, so she didn't complain. She took out her wallet and handed over a few notes.

She returned to the car and stood in the brilliant sunlight for a few minutes. She needed clarity and transparency after her time in the solicitor's office.

Chapter 18

Ava parked on the road near her mother's house, yet far enough away that her family would not see the car. She had developed a lack of trust that what they were doing was harmful, and she didn't want to be a part of their behavior.

She had just opened the door to leave the car when the phone rang. Ava sat down on the seat of the car and closed the car door shut again. "Hello," she said, answering a call where she didn't know the caller. The call was local, so she thought it must be someone she'd met. Nearly all her friends and coworkers were still enjoying London.

"Is this Miss Hedges?" the voice asked. It was a gruff and deep man's voice. It sounded familiar, but she couldn't place the voice.

"Speaking."

"This is Dr. Walsh from the hospital. Do you have a moment to talk? Are you somewhere where you'll be with someone?" The doctor's voice sounded serious.

Ava panicked. Doctors only called when something serious was involved. This was not a simple matter of a panic attack.

"I can talk. I'm alone, but that's fine." She cleared her throat and waited.

"It seems that you ingested a poison when you came into the hospital. There was a rather large dose of arsenic trioxide in your system. In today's world, that most likely comes from ingesting rat poison. Do you have a rodent problem at your house?"

"What? I don't know. I'm only visiting my family for a few

days following the death of my grandfather. I have no idea where someone might have gotten access to poison, much less how it would get in me." Ava felt panic, thinking that she could easily have been dead.

"I see. Then I'm going to have to ask you a series of questions. Have you had anything to eat or drink that was not consumed by the rest of the family?"

Ava sputtered. "How long would it take to affect me?" Her mind was running over the events of the day she went to the hospital. What had she had to eat and drink?

"Quickly," the doctor said. "Within two to four hours, you would feel side effects. Your symptoms matched up with the arsenic. Fortunately, we were able to flush out your system without much delay. So, there wasn't any damage to your organs. That was the purpose of the second set of lab work we requested. Arsenic can be harmful to the liver and kidneys."

All of this was coming quickly for Ava. She now understood why the doctor had asked about a second person's presence. She couldn't remember all the details from the doctor.

"But how?"

"Well, if there were no other person who had those symptoms in the household, then I would likely suspect that you were the lone target of the rat poison. That's not a good sign. If I were you, I would at least stop eating and drinking anything at your family's house. At best, I would move out. Do you need recommendations for a hotel or Airbnb? I can get my nurse to provide some, so you'd be safer there than in the family home."

Ava started to protest the man's comments, coming out and accusing her family of trying to kill her. However, she stopped before the first word came out. While the family had shared all the food, she was the only one to drink from that damned blue ceramic cup, the one her mother had made for her. Had her mother done that? She thought back to how proud her mother had been when she came home with the handmade cups, one for each of the children. She had painted their names on the cups so that she could keep them straight.

Ava thought back to all the times she'd had panic attacks as a child. Had this been the accurate diagnosis, or had she been poisoned – an answer that no doctor would have suspected without detailed testing?

"How long has this been going on?" Ava asked, fearing that she was right about the years of poisoning.

"Well, we did a small hair test while you were here. It appears that the poisoning started a few days ago. This was not your first poisoning incident, but it's limited to the past few days."

Ava thought about it. She hadn't been mistreated while in London. It was only in the past few days—since she arrived in York—that this had happened. Just the time when she stayed with her mother.

The doctor began again. "I will tell you on the bright side: the person who did this did not want you dead. The doses were such that you would be very ill and out of commission for a few days, but you would not die. You'd need a dose about one and a half times what you were given."

Ava wasn't sure if she should be relieved or worried. This killer could be waiting to give Ava the next dose at any time. How would she stay at her mother's house without consuming any food or drink?

"However," the doctor continued, "whoever has done this has been at it for a while. This is not the first time you've been dosed."

Ava thought back to her other panic attacks at her mother's house. She had thought they had been caused by nerves, the stress of being back in this house and with these people.

Instead, she learned that someone was trying to damage her, if not kill her.

"Excuse me, are you there? I know this is a huge shock, and I would have preferred to have done this in person—to ensure your mental health is intact, but I don't have you on the calendar until next week for a routine follow-up appointment, and I didn't think it could wait. I hope that's okay."

Ava took a deep breath. "That's fine. I'll be fine." She hung up before the doctor could speak again.

She was in shock. Ava recognised the emotion from all her experiences. Her mind wanted to rush to the significant question: who? Someone had put rat poison in her food or drink—and for what reason? She tried to focus on the who, but her mind kept saying, why?

The two things went together, and she couldn't understand how she could be the victim of a poisoning at the hands of a family member. Of course, her mother stood out as a potential perpetrator. She did the cooking, and she filled the drinks at the table. She even ensured the glasses were identified by their names on each one. She remembered when her mother had had the cups made—had she been poisoning her since then? Ava couldn't have been more than ten then, and she now wondered about the timing.

Perhaps this was all tied to the abuse as well. Could the poison have affected her memory? She would have to look into that. It would give Donna an excellent motive if it did.

Her brother was the next potential poisoner. He was so moody, so unpredictable, that Ava could imagine Luke poisoning the whole family if his mood was dark enough. But he didn't seem to have a motive. Ava tried to think of one, but no clear reasons existed. She supposed that he could have wanted her dead so he would be the only heir if their mother died.

Luke had seemed uncaring about his father's possible role as another heir to their grandfather's estate. Could he be planning to kill both Donna and their father once Ava was out of the way? She could easily see it.

And, of course, Vicki—Ava could easily see her aunt kill people just for the joy of it. She'd seen the woman lose her temper for the slightest thing. In a situation where hundreds of thousands of pounds were concerned, there was no telling what Vicki might do.

Ava paused and realised what she was doing. She was categorising everyone in the family as a potential poisoner who wanted Ava dead—or at least out of commission for the near future. The thought of her family wanting her out of the way made her cry.

She had always known that her mother was not quite right, and that the family was not normal. Her friends had two parents, and those parents did not criticise the children daily. She wondered again what it might have been like—what she might have been like—if she had grown up with those people.

Ava even went as far as to role-play the situation of being accepted and loved for who she was. Instead, she was now wondering who had made an attempt on her life – and who had set her up for abuse in the worst way.

Ava could not handle going home and pretending that everything was okay. She decided to spend the night at a hotel. There was no way that she could afford a hotel and its rates for the rest of her time in York, but she had more than enough funds to indulge one night away from home—and tonight was definitely that night.

The biggest fear that Ava had was running into someone who knew her and asking her what she was doing in a hotel when her mother owned two homes. Ava thought about that idea—staying at her grandfather's home, but Donna owned it or was close to possessing it. The thought of even staying in a house Donna owned was too much for her.

The receptionist was far too young to recognise Ava and handed her a key without comment. She only had clothes and a bag with her, so the receptionist gave her a few odd glances.

She went to the room and flopped down on the bed. When she awoke, it was nearly seven pm, and Ava was hungry. She ordered room service, nothing more than a burger and fries. She had already made a deal with herself that she would see no one in her family or friends tonight. It was simply too much to bear. Someone had tried to kill her.

Thinking back to the doctor's words, she could not see a distinction between an assault with poison and an attempted murder. In either case, someone had given her a dangerous drug that could have a lethal reaction. Even if the person had only wanted to hurt her, the result could have been the end of her.

The phone rang. It was Donna. Ava did nothing, just letting it go to voicemail. Donna called again and then a third time. Ava did not doubt that this was about control and not about any maternal concern for her daughter.

Within seconds, the phone rang again. Now Luke had called her, and Ava thought back to the last time Luke had called. He'd told her that their grandfather was dead. His voice then had been cold and distant. She wondered if he had been upset or if that was just a tone used per Donna's directions. She wished that she could have a better relationship with Luke, but now he was denying that the abuse had taken place at the Queen's Head pub. He said it never happened.

Ava finished her dinner and put the tray back outside the door. When she returned, the phone rang again. This time, it was a number that wasn't in her contacts, but she recognised it from the multiple calls—Mrs. Horridge.

Ava highly doubted that this caller had done so at her mother's request. The two women did not get along well.

She picked up the phone, and the other woman spoke immediately. "Ava, thank goodness. I've been trying to get in touch with you."

"Hello, Mrs. Horridge. Sorry, I've been busy with my grandfather's funeral and all." Ava did not want to get together with the woman now. She had no desire to explain her living arrangements tonight or her time in the hospital. Women in this town gossiped, and the news would get back to Donna soon enough.

"I know, dear, but it is related to that."

Ava furrowed her brow. That made no sense. Her older teacher had not been at the funeral, and she had seen nothing of her around the house. Ava couldn't imagine what the woman had to say about her grandfather.

"I don't understand," Ava started.

"Your mother was talking to a neighbour of mine. She indicated that your grandfather had not made a will, and therefore, the entire estate went to her and her sister. That's just not right."

Ava cleared her throat. She thought of Mr. Watkins and his answers to Ava's questions. Perhaps she could get the proof that he'd lied, and a will existed.

"That's very interesting," Ava said after a long pause. "Did someone tell you this?"

"No, dear. I was a witness to the will. I signed it."

Chapter 19

Ava hadn't slept much the night before, and after checkout, she thought it best to go home and confront the poisoning and the will. She now had a motive for a person to poison her. Mrs. Horridge explained that the will had been made a few months ago. Her grandfather had left a portion of his estate for his grandchildren. She and Luke got a sizable amount of money, and the rest was split between his two daughters, Donna and Vicki. The old teacher had been vague on the exact numbers or percentages, but she had been certain on the various bequests.

This made far more sense to Ava. The haste her mother was using to close the probate on the house and the money could be explained if she was not the only recipient of her grandfather's estate. The faster she got her hands on the money, the faster it could disappear and not be found—even if Ava could prove that it was stolen.

Ava stepped inside her mother's house and hoped no one was home. She was still angry—furious—that her mother was so underhanded.

How could she have been so wrong about the woman? Ava had always thought of her as a bit slow but caring at some level. Now that she was looking at her mother with an adult's eyes, she knew better.

"Where have you been all night?" came her mother's voice from the next room. "I'm sure I know. You and that shrink were out carousing all night. Don't you know better than to give it away that way? What am I saying? I know you've had plenty of experience."

"You don't know anything about me," Ava said. "Nothing."

Donna did not respond, only laughed at her daughter's words.

Ava could feel the blood rush to her face and head. Her heart was pounding, and her mouth was dry. She wanted to scream. "But I know all about you."

Donna put the grocery bags down on the counter and fumbled momentarily with her back to Ava. She wasn't sure what her mother was doing.

When Donna turned around, she had a serrated utility knife in her hand. Ava did not like the way that this argument was going. "Why don't you put that down, and we can talk?" Ava suggested taking a step back.

"You're not afraid of a silly knife, are you?" Donna said. She touched her pointer finger against the tip of the blade. It looked very sharp from Ava's perspective. Donna pulled her finger away quickly, highlighting her suggestion.

"Mother, please put that down," Ava repeated.

"Now it's mother. Before you called me 'Donna.'" She took a step towards Ava again. "So, what do you know about me? Let's talk and iron this all out. We can cut through the BS."

Ava suspected that "cut" was a well-chosen word. Her mother had not put the knife down, and as such, she'd maintained superiority over her daughter. Ava tried to run her mind through the kitchen cabinets, seeing if she could think of any item that could protect her. The problem was that she hadn't lived here in years. So, she had no idea what types of knives or lids or pots and pans were there. She needed another knife or a large lid to help her.

She kept her neck straight and her eyes on Donna. She didn't want to give away what she was trying to do mentally.

Ava hoped that she could have the element of surprise.

"Don't think of where the knives are," Donna said. "I moved them when I found this little cutie. Isn't it pretty?" Donna said. "I got this at a car boot sale. I doubt that anyone would know that I have something that could be so dangerous. But it's only me and your brother—and right now he's out. There's no one to worry about—except you."

Ava thought about screaming, but how would that help? The neighbours would not know what was going on. They might come over, but Donna could dispatch them as well as Ava. Her phone was in her pocket, but if she fumbled with it, Donna would know what she was attempting to accomplish.

If she could distract Donna for a few seconds, then she might get her phone activated and she could press the dial button to get someone to hear what was going on. However, distractions would be hard to come by, especially because her mother had a knife in her hand. What would she do then?

"So, what did you want to talk to me about?" Donna asked. "Maybe something the doctor told you when he called?"

Ava froze. How had her mother known of that? Had she talked to him? Would she know that Ava was on to her?

"He called here and said he needed to speak to you in a matter of life and death. I thought that perhaps he was going to tell you something about what you ate. Then you'd suspect your dear mother of harming you." Donna set her hand on the counter with the knife gleaming in the morning sunlight. Perhaps she was getting tired, Ava thought.

"He did," Ava said. "He told me that someone had poisoned me at dinner that evening. The poison was fast acting, so it had to be at dinner."

"And how did I do that?" asked Donna. "After all, everyone ate the same food. We all had portions out of the same bowl. What type of killer am I where I can make only one person get sick?"

Ava hadn't thought of this in detail, and she had to agree that her mother had served all the food in bowls, meaning they'd all eaten the meal.

"Miss Smarty-Pants, you hadn't thought of that. You'd immediately jumped to the conclusion that I'd been responsible for your poor health. You've had these attacks since you were a child. All those years of poisoning my own child. Is that what you think of me?"

Ava would have been far more convinced if her mother had put the knife on the counter. However, she still held it tight in her fist. Ava could see her mother's white knuckles as she held it tightly.

"The drinks. You have a drink for me, a special drink."

Donna laughed. "Do you think I made that for you, my little precious girl so that I could pour poison into it? So, I could kill you?"

"The doctor said that it wasn't enough to kill me, just enough to make me sick," Ava recalled. " You wouldn't be killing me."

Ava tried to speak, but the knife was now being held out like a teacher's pointing stick. She was making her point with a sharp-edged knife. " All this drama and no one wanted to kill you. No one wanted you dead. So now what?"

"You're up to something. I don't know what and why yet, but you have something up your sleeve."

Donna laughed and then thrust the knife at her like a fencing master. "You have nothing. You don't know what I'm doing, according to you, and you don't know why I'm doing it. You don't like me, so you want me to be the villain of the piece. I've never done anything that you could put a finger on. I'm innocent of all charges. Just your hatred of me."

"But the abuse. Luke remembers the abuse, too."

Donna tapped the edge of the knife on her cheek as she would a finger. "Does he? He told me yesterday that he didn't believe any of it was true. You'd been pushing him to say it happened, but he doesn't recall a thing."

Ava was stunned at how fast Luke had changed his story. He had brought her into this and then dumped her with the repercussions. "I've found out where it was done. It's a new pub now, but I found it, and I've been there. I've seen it."

"I don't like this. It's one thing to think me stupid or weak, but now you think I'm a criminal. A woman who hurts her children. You've gone too far this time."

Ava took two steps back. Donna's tone and her facial expression had both changed. Her face had an aggressive appearance, and her eyes carried hatred for her daughter. Her voice had grown nasty and sarcastic. She wasn't sure what Donna was capable of now, but it scared her.

"Can't we talk this out?" Ava asked. She felt that she had run up against the counter. The amount of room to escape was getting smaller. She hoped that Luke would come downstairs, but would he save her? He'd already sold her out by telling her about the abuse but denying everything when the time for action came.

"What is there to talk about? You think I poisoned you, that I wanted to kill you. What else is there?" Donna was agitated now, and she swung the knife from side to side. "You've always been this way. Paranoid and crazy. I never wanted you." A harshness flashed through Donna's eyes. "You were an accident, and you ruined my whole life."

Ava grew angry. Her mother had said this to her many times in the past. When the topic became too difficult or involved Donna's wrongdoing, she would blame the entire situation on Ava's mental health.

"I'm not crazy, and I'm not paranoid." Despite her

assurances, she felt like a small girl again who was trying to make a comeback to stop her mother from making other accusations. She decided to give her mother a jolt, something to stall time and perhaps allow Ava to escape. "I know about the will, don't I? Is that crazy? Maybe that's why you want me dead. I know too much."

The look on her mother's face turned from aggressive to frightened. The expression only lasted a moment or two, but Ava knew enough about the woman that she knew she'd struck a nerve. Something was up with her grandfather's will.

"You don't know anything," Donna said. She kept swinging the knife back and forth, but she took another step closer. "Anything I did, I did for you. Though goodness knows why, you always come out smelling of roses."

The phrase took Ava out of focus. Why had her mother said that to her so many years ago? What had she meant? Was Donna jealous of her daughter and her potential? Was she angry if she'd known that Ava got part of her grandfather's estate? Or was it just that Ava was free of family responsibilities? She wondered what had caused her to say it now.

"Why do you say that? I had my rough times," Ava said, hoping she could extend this long enough for someone to help her—or cause a distraction that would allow her to escape. Maybe Luke would come around. Even Vicki throwing slurs at her would be welcome if Ava could get out of this kitchen without being cut.

"Right, a good home, a good family, food to eat, clothes to wear. That's a tough life for sure."

"But—" Ava started before Donna shouted at her.

"Are you going to bring up that abuse again? The abuse that no one else remembers. Is that what you were going to say?" The words grew louder. Certainly, someone in the neighbourhood had to hear the screeches as Donna shouted.

Ava put her hands over her ears. The sound was piercing.

"I did nothing wrong." Donna stamped her foot like a child, a very angry child with a knife in her hand.

She looked at Ava and stood up straight. "Now look what you've done," she said. "Why did you have to come home? Why didn't you stay away? You should have figured it out that Luke called you. I didn't call you. I didn't want you—I never wanted you – you were an accident remember."

Ava took a deep breath. The comment hurt. She remembered these tantrums from her youth, her mother screaming and carrying on. They usually ended with a slap across the face or a gut punch. Today, Ava was worried that it could be far worse.

For all those times when Ava was afraid of her mother's unpredictable behavior, she'd never feared for her life. Today, she was worried that Donna could go farther—so much farther. Ava wondered if her mother could kill her.

Last night, she'd been confused about the doctor's statements about her family and the threat of the poison. She couldn't fathom the idea that a family member could harm her. This conversation had recalled all the time that they *had* hurt her, physically and mentally.

Now, with the stakes so much higher, she feared that the damage could be far worse.

Donna took another two steps closer to her daughter. "Now, where were we before you made those crazy comments?" Donna was within arm's length now, and the knife was still swinging back and forth. Once, it grazed Ava's arm, but it didn't cut her. The mere feeling of it was enough to make Ava ill.

Chapter 20

The kitchen door to the back garden opened, and Ava spun to look. George was standing there, looking at the scenario. "Hello. I heard voices and thought I'd try the back door." He smiled at both of them.

Donna glared at him. "You're not welcome in my house. Leave now. You already dumped my daughter. What business do you have here?"

"I invited him," Ava said. She squeezed past her mother and slipped into George's arms.

"I did get your message," he said. He squeezed her tightly, perhaps to let her know she was safe now.

"Can we put the knife down and talk?" George said. He was using the voice that Ava had heard when they had talked about abuse and families. The calm, gentle tone that made people feel at ease.

Donna looked at the knife and then beamed at George. "Of course, Ava just startled me when I was getting ready to make dinner. I was frightened and held on to the knife when I turned around. You can never be too careful," she added.

"She was going to kill me. She had tried to kill me. The doctor called. He told me that I'd been poisoned. Not a big enough dose to kill me, but enough to harm my organs. I think she was trying to scare me into leaving, and I think she wanted to break us up."

Donna laughed. "I think you'll have your hands full with this one. She's been crazy ever since she was a child. People were trying to kill her. She was abused. I drove her father away," Donna said. She continued the litany of accusations against Ava. The worst part was that every one of them was true. Ava had said these things, but not without proof. She had doctors' reports that she had been poisoned. She had Mrs. Horridge's word about the will. Her father was gone.

George squeezed her hand and looked at Donna. "Well, the first thing we need to do is reduce this level of aggression. It's always best to talk peacefully. Ava will stop making accusations, and Donna, you can put down the knife. Then we can talk about what's going on here."

Donna looked at him. Her mouth was set in a straight line, and her eyes were squinting. Ava wasn't sure George's tranquil words would have the desired effect. Her mother hesitated momentarily and then set the weapon down on the counter.

Without qualms, George walked over to the knife and put it in his pocket. The sheath, sticking out of his jacket, was a reminder of what had just happened. Her mother was a threat to her—and possibly others.

"Now, let's talk about this. Donna, I hear that you don't like what Ava said this morning. What did you not like? The tone, the content?" George continued for a few minutes, asking Donna questions she wouldn't answer.

Finally, she looked at the couple and stormed out of the room. Ava had a slight fear that her mother would come back with a gun or another weapon to harm her—and maybe George as well.

"Can we go somewhere else? Please," Ava pleaded. She heard the panic in her voice, but she couldn't make it stop. Her hand trembled in George's steady fingers.

"Have you been staying here? Even after you were poisoned?" George asked.

Ava told him how she had moved most of her things out and was staying at a hotel for the moment, though she couldn't afford it for much longer.

"I think I should just get a train and head back to London. Nothing good is going to come from this. I've nearly been killed twice: with the poison and today with the knife. I am not sure who did the first one, but today was Donna."

George smiled at her. "I saw it today. There's no question about it."

"That's the thing. I have witnesses to each of the events she mentioned. However, each one is a different witness, so it feels disjointed."

George laughed. "I would think that makes the case stronger. You don't have one person feeding you stories. You have several people who are corroborating your account. It's much harder to get a group of people to build a case. It's far easier to get one person to back you up—like Luke does for your mother."

As Ava heard the mention of her mother, her steely reserve began to melt like butter. All this in the last twenty-four hours had been too much for her. She'd never expected that her mother would harm her. She began to cry, and George squeezed her a bit tighter. It felt good to have the support of another person, someone outside the family who could see what a mess it was and listen to her complaints.

After a few minutes, George handed her a tissue. Ava had no idea where he'd procured such a thing. He hadn't moved an inch. She stood up straight and dabbed at her eyes.

"Feeling better?" George asked. "If so, perhaps we should get your things and leave before someone comes downstairs. I think you've had enough drama for the day."

Ava began to weep again, thinking of the chance of meeting her mother upstairs or Luke, who was now lying and covering for his mother. The betrayal was nearly as bad as the knife threat.

George sighed. "Tell you what. You go out and sit in the car. Turn on the engine and turn on the radio. Lock the doors. Do not answer or lower the windows unless I come to the door. Now, what do you need?"

She listed a small set of items. Ava hadn't brought much, as she hadn't planned on staying this long. She started crying again, missing the people she knew in London, where no one wanted to slice her into bits or feed her rat poison.

Despite these thoughts, she followed George's instructions to the letter. And waited. Ava was certain that her mother had done away with George when he came out of the house. Ava breathed a sigh of relief and unlocked the driver's door for him.

"So where to?" George said, not even addressing if anything had happened inside with her family.

Ava sniffed loudly, not wanting to cry again. The truth was that she had thought about sleeping in the rental car. Or asking the hospital for a room until she determined when to go back to London. She couldn't afford the hotel for many more nights, and at the same time, she had no close friends after all these years. It would be impossible to impose on them. And George had just popped up in her life again after leaving her for her mother's machinations.

He looked at her and gave her a sigh. "No place to go, eh? Tell you what, the roommate is out of town for the near future."

Ava wasn't sure what the roommate had to do with anything. "And?"

"You could stay with me—for a while."

Ava sat up straight in her seat. What was he proposing, and why was a man who lived by communicating so bloody bad at it?

At least George seemed to recognise that he'd erred. His face blushed a little as he cleared his throat and began again. "Look, not like that. We're just getting reacquainted after your mother's stunt—and your work dealing with the past. I was meaning, you know. There's a spare bedroom, the roommate's room, until further notice. It would be a platonic stay. I don't think it's a fantastic idea for us to jump into a physical relationship yet. But I don't think you're safe there."

"Especially around mealtimes," Ava said, hearing her own sarcasm in the tone.

George laughed, but Ava realised in his weak chuckle that he hadn't heard about the incident at the hospital. He knew she'd been admitted and stayed there for two nights, but not the cause of the visit. So, she spent the time driving across town to explain what she'd met.

George's reaction was startling. Ava was expecting him to be casual and calm like he was in this therapy voice, but he was angry. After a few minutes of swearing and venom in his tone, George seemed to calm down. Now, it was his turn to take a deep breath. "Sorry about that. I'm an idiot. Have you ever heard of Munchausen syndrome by proxy, or as it's sometimes called, Factitious disorder by proxy?"

Ava shook her head. "Is that something I have?"

George shook his head vehemently. "I heard what Donna said. You're not crazy. You don't have a mental illness that I can see. This one is all on her. It's a type of child abuse."

"Could this be related to what happened in the pub's cellar?"

"No, it's not. It's when the mother uses her children to get attention. The way it's done is to give the child fake illnesses by inducing the symptoms of the diseases. Donna wanted you to suffer from anxiety disorders, so she gave you a poison that gave you gastro disorders, so your throat hurt, your stomach ached, you threw up."

Ava thought back to the unexplained anxiety attacks, the ones that had left her sick. Each time, her mother had taken Ava to the doctor and spent long periods with the medical staff. Had she just wanted attention? From what she'd seen and heard today, anything was possible.

"Is there a cure for that?" Ava asked, wondering if Donna could be fixed in some way.

"It's a form of child abuse, and the typical response is to move the child away from his or her mother. I think the same recommendations should be applied. Stay away from her."

Chapter 21

"This is silly," Ava said as she sat on George's couch. She'd been there three days at this point. If her family knew where she was, they had made no attempts to contact her. Ava appreciated the silence and the time to get her own thoughts and emotions under control.

However, George had come home today with something that had floored her. Somehow, he had obtained her grandfather's medical records. He'd explained that he'd wanted to see if there were any signs of poisoning in his records.

Ava flopped down onto the sofa while he spoke. It was bad enough that Donna had inflicted these things on Ava, but now George was saying that the woman might have killed others as well. The idea that her mother was a serial killer was beyond her.

"What is this?" Ava asked, looking at the stack of papers. They had her grandfather's name across several of them, Arthur Farley. She flipped through several of them, but she couldn't understand the words used or the drugs and diagnoses.

"These are the records for your grandfather, surrounding the time of his death. I'll go through this in a few minutes." He dialed a nearby restaurant that Ava enjoyed and ordered a delivery. She appreciated the thoughtfulness.

He sat down next to her and picked up the first folder. "I've already been through this once and know what the folders say. It's not good news. But I want you to have all the details too. It's the only way that you can combat your family, should we use this data."

"Was he poisoned? Did Donna kill him too?"

"Let's start at the beginning and go through it. Like I said, I want you to see the details. I want you to know what the medical terms mean. No autopsy was done. Your grandfather was under a physician's care. He was elderly. He had multiple organ failure. In short, he wasn't expected to live much longer."

Ava looked at George. "Then why kill him?"

George shrugged. "It could be that your mother and her sister just got tired of waiting. Some people, especially those with their own mental illnesses, might not have the ability to wait for what they want. So, they lash out and take it. This situation is much more worrisome. Your mother is far sneakier in her killing. That might come from the fact that she poisoned you for years. She knew how to get the other person to ingest it."

"How does that help us?"

"Well, it doesn't mean we can call Father Brown or Poirot and have them solve the case. This is real life, so we're looking at a case that—may be a murder. That's the best we can hope for."

"Then what are we looking for?" Ava asked, feeling somewhat disappointed. Now that she knew about her mother and the poisoning, there was nothing more she wanted than to put her in prison for as long as she could.

"The first thing I noticed is that there were traces of alcohol in his system. The nurse could smell it on his breath. So, we don't know how much he'd had, but he'd had some. What types of booze did he drink?" George asked.

Ava admired him at that moment. He was helping someone he'd recently met. He was all into the research and documents, hoping to get any clues that he could. He was kind and generous with his time.

"Are you with me?" George asked, looking slightly confused.

Ava didn't want to tell him what she'd been thinking. The arrangement of sharing the flat but living in the roommate's room had worked out so far.

"His favorite drink was Guinness." Ava tried to make it look like she'd been paying attention. She'd selected his comments on alcohol, so she had thrown out a trivia fact to help the research.

"That wasn't what I asked, but okay. A dark stout has a strong flavor, and obviously, you can't see anything in the stout, so it would be an ideal way to get him to drink the poison. He wouldn't taste it or see it. He'd never have known. Had he been having any of the same symptoms you complained about?" George looked at her with enthusiasm.

"I don't know for sure. I hadn't talked to him in ages. I hadn't talked to anyone from York in a long time. I wanted to be as far from here as I could be." Ava was paying attention now, and it made her uncomfortable to say this. She didn't want to spill her intentions to leave York as soon as she could. There was a spark of a rapport here, and she didn't know how George would take it if she told him that this relationship had a sell-by date.

He cleared his throat as if he hadn't noticed the implications of her comment. "Can you get me the blue folder there?"

Ava handed it to him, and George began to flip through the pages. "Here we go. Your grandfather had issues with vomiting and stomach aches. I mean, it could be entirely unrelated to your poison, but it seems a bit too much."

Ava sighed. "It could be, but it's not enough to put her in jail. I mean, I don't have enough to put her away for what she did to me. There's certainly not enough evidence to arrest her for grandfather's death."

George looked down at the floor. Ava had no idea if he was disappointed about her comments about leaving or the weak case that could never be proved. " What more would we need to get a conviction in this case?"

Ava ticked off the pieces of a trial that were so often mentioned in the crime shows she watched. "Motive, means, and opportunity."

" Does Donna have those?" George said.

"Of course she does. Grandfather had tons of money, and she wanted it. But that applies to anyone."

"Not really; the only two who benefited were Donna and Vicki. You and Luke can be struck down for motive. He didn't leave you a penny."

Ava thought about Mrs. Horridge's comments to her again. She'd shared them with George on the same day when Donna had come after her with a knife. There could be a motive for Ava and Luke if they had thought that they would receive a large share of the estate. How would they know that their mother had taken it?

Ava explained this again, and George nodded. "You're right, of course. What about the means?"

"As far as I know, only Donna had arsenic, and she'd used it for other people. So that fits. But again, it would have been in the house or the land around it. So, anyone could have it. This is getting tedious," Ava said, feeling glum.

"And opportunity?"

"I don't know when grandfather passed away. Luke called me one night and just told me that he'd passed away. No details at all."

George picked up a file and flipped through the pages. "Here it is."

Ava looked at the page and saw that the old man had

passed away three days before Luke had called Ava.

"What took him so long to call?" George asked.

"I am going to guess that my mother didn't want me to attend, but Luke defied her and called me after a battle."

George smiled. "I'm glad he did call you. I got to meet you this way."

While it seemed like an awkward moment—discussing the death of a family member, Ava felt that same spark she'd felt earlier. She leaned over and gave George a kiss. She was shocked at George's passion in those first seconds. She had expected a small peck, given the fact that they were reading through her grandfather's medical records, but George had apparently felt the same magic that she had.

They broke away after a few seconds, and George grinned at her. "In all my time reviewing records, I've never had this happen before."

Ava raised an eyebrow. "Are you unhappy that I broke your record?"

He laughed. "Not at all. I'm glad, but I still think we should go slow."

"I've been wanting to do that for a few days now, so I'm thinking that's pretty slow. But I agree, though I think you might have waited ten minutes or so to bring up the subject of going slow."

George blushed and then looked down at the floor. "Let's just say that I am finding it difficult to sleep because I'm thinking of you."

Now, it was Ava's time to turn red. "Same here. And now that we're both embarrassed, let's get back to work. How do we find out the opportunity?"

"Now that we have a date and time of his death, then we can ask the others when they saw Arthur last before his death. That would give us an idea of who was there recently. And we don't know who called 999 for him. The paperwork doesn't say. That would be a good place to start."

Ava picked up her phone. "I'm going to ask Luke what he knows. He's the only one still talking to me, so let's start there."

Luke arrived at George's flat thirty minutes later. "No one knew where you were," he said.

He looked around the flat and smiled. "And you complained about me, selling myself out. I'm sure this is worth it."

Ava tried to ignore him, but she felt a flash of anger. She wanted to protest and argue, but he was here for a purpose. No reason to let his assumptions rile her up.

"I like it here," Ava replied, trying to keep the conversation light without discussing the abuse. She had another topic in mind. "Who found grandfather when he died?"

Luke laughed. "I should have known you had a reason to ask me here. Family bonding and such is just a ruse to get me here and pump me. Do you think that grandfather was killed by someone in the family? Who knows? Did you call me here to confront me with your so-called evidence and get me to confess?" He laughed again, and the sound was not his usual guffaw. He looked serious—and angry.

"I'm not accusing anyone of anything, Luke," she started. "But if someone could poison me—and the doctors tell me I was given rat poison—then someone could have killed grandfather too."

Luke shook her head. "Look, I get that you're upset. You're just getting used to these flashbacks. They're painful, they're scary, but that doesn't mean that the family had anything to do with it. I had nothing to do with it, and I'm a family member. Hell, I'm just as upset about the abuse as anyone. And I understand you want to lash out and hurt someone because you've been hurt, too." He looked over at George and nodded.

"Isn't that right? You're a head shrink –you can tell her."

George cleared his throat and looked at Ava. She understood that he was in a bad position. Luke was talking superficially, whereas George knew Ava better than most anyone ever had.

"Ah, figures," Luke continued. "He's not going to back me up. He's on your side. It's still true, even if you have him convinced. No one is trying to kill you. No one is trying to hurt you. Bad things happened in the past, but now you have to learn to cope with them. Work with someone and get past the anger. I did."

Ava watched George, seeing what he thought about Luke's comments and his suggestion that he had participated in therapy at some point. While she would never say it, the fact that Luke had tried to end his own life suggested that he wasn't totally healed from his wounds.

"I won't believe it until you have proof—hard solid can't be denied proof." With that, he stormed out of the room, slamming the door behind him.

"What did you think about that?" Ava asked, wanting a professional opinion on her brother. While she didn't want to be analysed by George, she was fine with him studying the other members of her family.

"Lots of stuff is going on there. I'm not sure what to make of it. On the one hand, he's feeling fairly confident, but then, a few days ago, he attempted suicide, which does fit with the rest of that. I think there must be a great deal of denial."

Ava nodded. "We still didn't get the information we needed. I have no idea where each person was on the day of my grandfather's death. It would help. The poison acted fast. I do remember that from all the chaos that night. So, they would have to be there just a few hours before."

George bit his lip, which Ava had discovered was a sure

sign that he was going to disagree with her. "Not necessarily. The person would need access to food and drink before the event. I mean, let's assume it's in your grandfather's stout. Someone comes over and finds a container with twelve drinks in it. He—or she—picks one, takes off the cap, and puts the poison in it. Then they put the cap back on, and no one ever knows what happened. The killer doesn't have to be within miles of the crime."

"So, it didn't have to be Donna or Luke the night I was poisoned. Someone else could have put the poison in the food days before the event. That would mean Vicki's back in the mix, even though she wasn't around."

"The problem with your poisoning is twofold. First, they didn't want to kill you. Why? Just to get you out of the way?"

"Or you might be a threat, and they wanted to keep us apart. That worked well for the person."

George blushed a little. "I doubt I'm important enough to want me out of the way."

"But you know about abuse and things like that. You might spot something that gives it away." Ava smiled.

"That's possible, but the same applies to you. The poisoning put you in the hospital for days. That meant you couldn't see what was going on at the house. Maybe Donna or one of the others was making moves to get the house or the estate or something else that we don't know about."

"But I don't know how the poison was administered," Ava said. "I ate what they ate. I drank what they drank. How do we explain that?"

George took her into his arms. "When we answer those two questions, we'll know who is behind all of this."

Chapter 22

Ava shot out of bed, screaming. She looked around, and for a moment, she had no idea where she was. After a few seconds, she realised she was in the spare room at George's flat.

The flashback had been so intense tonight. Perhaps it was the discussions they'd had over the past few nights that brought this on. The experience was like a movie without sound.

George came into the room without knocking. "Are you okay?" he asked.

Ava couldn't help but notice that he was only wearing the bottoms of his pajamas. For someone who sat and listened all day, he was remarkably in good shape. His arms were thick, and she could see the rounded muscles above his elbows. He didn't have six-pack abs, but his stomach was flat, and his pecs were rounded too. She'd have to ask about that when she wasn't on the edge of an anxiety attack.

"Not really. Sorry to wake you. It was just another flashback—the same as before, but nothing new. I felt like I couldn't breathe. Then the scream came out. I wasn't sure if I was dreaming it or it was real."

George laughed. "It was real. The neighbours probably heard it in their flats."

The flashbacks had stopped including more information. There were no additional details about the place, the adults, or the children. The focus now was on Ava—how she felt and how much pain she was in. The emotions were getting more powerful. She wished they would go away, but this week, they had been every night.

"Was there any more information that came from them?" George asked. He had been helping her keep a diary of the dreams.

"Just the same as yesterday and the day before. I'm seeing more faces of children, but that doesn't help. I can't find an adult based on the face of a child. The only one I recognise is Luke, which is only because I grew up with him. That's it. Is there something that can be done to push this forward? I feel like my flashbacks are stuck in one place."

"That's why I suggested keeping a diary. This might help bring your memories back, and you'll be able to see more. I worry because that is usually a painful breakthrough. I don't want you to have to go through that alone." George put his hand over hers as they talked.

Ava's phone rang, even though it was only 8 am. She answered it, but she didn't recognise the number.

"Ava, this is Mr. Watkins. Do you have time this morning to meet? I think we need to talk." His voice had the same tone, but there was a breathless urgency to his speech.

"What time would you like me to come to your office?" Ava said, having an odd feeling that this was important.

"Would now be acceptable?" he asked.

Ava looked at George and said, "Certainly."

Ava had not bothered to shower or dress for a meeting with the solicitor. She had found clothes that were not too wrinkled. She had not brought nearly enough clothing since she had expected only to stay a few days.

She and George had disagreed on whether he should attend the meeting with her. As a therapist, he had worried that this was a bombshell, meaning she would need support. Ava considered but had fears that the solicitor would not open up with witnesses in the room.

They had compromised by having George drive her there

but stay in the car in the carpark.

Ava opened the door and went into the solicitor's office. He sat at his desk, which was strewn with papers. He looked up and gave her a weak smile. Ava wondered what he'd learned that made him behave in this manner. It had to be bad.

"I came as fast as I could," Ava said, sitting in one of the two seats in front of his desk. "You said you had news?"

He cleared his throat. "Yes, you had asked me to find someone to tease out the owners of the Queen's Head pub. As you recall, multiple shell companies seemed to mask the true owners' names."

Ava nodded, feeling that this was not needed. She already knew what she had asked the solicitor to do.

"My agent has done so," he said. "I feel that I need to go through this with you, level by level, so there's no confusion about what I'm saying." He pulled a bundle of papers from one of the many stacks and flipped through them until he found what he wanted.

"This is the ownership of the Queen's Head. It's registered as a corporation that began only a few months before it 'purchased' the Queen's Head. You can see, this seems to indicate that this was not done as the result of being purchased by an existing company, but more as a way to hide the owner's real identities."

Ava looked at the paper and nodded. She wished he could hurry up. She could feel the energy in her, making her want to take the papers and read them herself.

They went through four more layers of shell companies until Mr. Watkins came to the last page. "When my agent came back with this final level, I made him check his results. It didn't seem to make sense."

He slipped the page over to Ava. She took it and read it carefully. Ava couldn't understand why he was so cautious about this matter.

Until she read it.

The paper showed the owners of the fifth shell company, Arthur Farley, her grandfather, and another man named Alfred Cook. Ava didn't know the second name, but she damned sure knew the first.

"How much do I owe you?" Ava asked without batting an eye. "And may I have a copy of these papers?"

Mr. Watkins quoted a reasonable price for the job. Ava was unused to the lower cost of living here in York. A solicitor in London would have charged twice that much. He cleared his throat. "Are you sure that you want these —"

Ava cut him off before he could finish. "I want a copy of these papers. I paid for them, and I'd like to have the evidence I requested."

The man nodded and went to make copies.

Ava focused on other things rather than what she'd just learned. She was certainly glad that George had come with her. Right now, she felt like she would burst open at any second. The knowledge was devastating. Ava could not imagine that her grandfather, along with a man named Cook, was behind all of this.

Ava knew that she would have to find Mr. Cook and then find out what he knew about her grandfather, the pub, and its heinous past. That would be her first order of business.

Mr. Watkins came back and handed her the papers. "Is there anything else I can help you with?" he asked.

Ava shook her head and then held out her hand. "No, you've been very helpful as it stands. I appreciate it."

Ava walked back to the car, again trying to push all of those thoughts away. She knew things would be better if George were there to talk to her and make sense of it.

She got into the car, looked at George, and burst into tears.

"It went well, I see?" George said after a minute of her crying.

Ava laughed as the tears still ran down her face. "You might say that. My grandfather was the owner of the Queen's Head. He and another man, Alfred Cook, were in cahoots. They used five layers of shell companies to hide their identities. They knew what they were doing, and they tried to cover it up."

"They didn't do a good job if the clerk found it this quickly."

Ava tried to smile, but it wasn't easy. "That's the wonder of the internet. Documents are put online, and the information can be found in a minute rather than a week of trying to hunt down the papers."

"Wow, so what does that mean?" George asked, waving at all the papers.

"My grandfather was behind the entire series of companies that were created so he and this other man could build a child abuse ring that likely made him a great deal of money — money that my mother seems to be stealing from the rest of the family." She looked at George. "This has to be the most convoluted family story you've ever heard."

He crinkled his nose as if he smelled something foul. "It's definitely top ten."

"I'll make it worse. If my grandfather hosted these abusive events, then he likely was a part of them. It means that Luke and I were likely abused by our own grandfather. It also means that Donna was involved. There's no way that he could have taken us for days and that she would not have known what was happening. She was a part of this, too."

George nodded. "Well, that's a lot of assumptions. In many cases with a family, other members will ignore what's happening, or they choose to overlook what is going on. It's a way of maintaining plausible denial. It's made all the more likely because your grandfather seemed to have the family purse strings."

Ava couldn't believe her mother would sell them out for a few pounds. Donna had ignored their plight, the flashbacks, and the other signs of abuse just for some money. It made Ava more certain that Donna had done something with the estate.

"Could that explain the situation with Luke?" Ava asked. She didn't understand the way that he denied Ava's memories after bringing them to his attention.

"Yes, in many cases of abuse, the child will try to please the parent in whatever way possible to make the abuse stop. So, they will do whatever the adult wants them to do. It would account for the way that he changed his mind. He's not sure of what his mother wants, so his account changed once he finds out what she wanted."

Ava's stomach roiled. The thought of family members abusing her was more than she could take. She put her head on the headrest and closed her eyes. Maybe if she pushed the thoughts away, things would get better.

"It will take a while to process all of this," he said.

"This is why you wanted to come with me?" she asked. "You thought I might find out something horrible? If you did, you were absolutely correct."

"I hate to tell you this, but so many cases of abuse are perpetrated by a family member. Given some comments and behaviors, I thought this might be the case here."

"What do we do?" Ava asked. She wanted to cry, but not now, not in front of George. It all felt like too much at the moment. She wanted some time to herself where she could mesh the flashbacks with what she'd learned. Perhaps she could make sense of this and then do what needed to be done for her own sake. However, she had no idea what that might be. Should she find out the truth from Luke, or should she look into the question of the will, or should she take Donna on face-to-face?

"What are you thinking?" George asked her.

"I'm wondering about my choices and how I should go about this. I have never been in a situation where—as an adult—I did not know what to do. This is probably the most important set of decisions I've ever had to make, and I'm clueless." Much as she tried, Ava couldn't help herself. She began to cry softly, and as she sat there, it became louder, and the tears flowed stronger.

"Let's get you home and see what we can do together," George said, turning on the car. "We can talk this all out."

The words, meant to be comforting, did nothing for her. She felt that this was the end of the road. She was a stereotype of abused children, and now that she knew it, the future held nothing for her. Not even George, with his compassion and caring, would want someone as damaged as this.

She continued to weep as they made it back to George's flat. George made tea for them and took it to Ava, who sat in a chair by herself. "Thank you. I don't know why you're so kind to me. I'm a wreck."

"You asked early how you could begin to handle all these situations. Would you like my suggestions, or would you prefer that I just listen?" George sat on the edge of the loveseat as he talked. He put this tea on the end table and observed her.

Ava hated that she felt like she was being analysed, but right now, she needed help, no matter how it came to her. "I guess I'd like to hear what you have to say," she said. She found another tissue and dabbed at her eyes. She was one of those unlucky people who followed a crying jag with a headache, like the one she was getting now. Ava took another sip of tea.

"Very well, if it were up to me, I'd start with the will and the estate. You already have information from Mrs. Horridge.

You could talk to a solicitor and see what could be done. It doesn't involve your mother or your brother, and they could be saved for another time when you're feeling stronger. This is a big blow to you, and you shouldn't pretend it's not."

"I don't know anything about the law. I only have the word of one woman, and that's it."

"We can find out who drew up the will. Then you can go from there. York doesn't have a million solicitors like London. We could knock it out in a day or so." George's tone was quiet and encouraging, but it had a sense of urgency. Maybe he wanted to help her, Ava thought, but she also wondered if he was interested in the estate. If her grandfather had indeed been running an abuse ring, he would likely have tons of money. He could have made all of them pay, or he would tell the police about their activities. The blackmail potential alone would have been worth a fortune. After all this, she had trouble trusting others, especially those close to her.

Chapter 23

Ava started calling solicitors at 10 a.m. the next morning. Despite George's assurance, there were numerous businesses in the York area, presuming that her grandfather had his will drawn up locally. The task went slowly, and by lunchtime, Ava was certain that this was a fool's errand.

However, she had no other ideas or paths to go down. She wasn't ready for her family, just as George had said. That would need to come later after she felt more confident in herself.

She was about to give up for the day when her last phone call paid off. The firm, Borden & White, was one of the trendier legal firms in York. Ava was a tad shocked, given that she'd never seen her grandfather care about trends or popularity. However, she had to admit that she knew little about her grandfather's actual life.

Ava went through her usual spiel about how she was calling regarding her family's situation. Her mother had lost the previous will. They had no copies, and their grandfather had passed away this week. As far as Ava knew, this was likely true. Her mother was hiding the will, and he had passed away. She knew from one of the witnesses, Mrs. Horridge, that he'd had their firm draw up the will.

"I'm so sorry for your loss," the man said. "I hadn't heard of the death, and we do have some filing to do now that he's passed. Could you bring me a copy of the death certificate, and I'll do the rest?"

Ava agreed with a smile, feeling she might get some

answers from the solicitor.

Borden & White Legal Services was far enough away that Ava had to drive. George had appointments all day, though he had offered to cancel those sessions. Ava had told him no, saying she needed to handle this herself. Plus, it would go over better if she was there alone, handling her grandfather's estate.

Ava had decided to wear the same black dress she'd worn to the funeral. She needed to appear bereft if she was going to get some answers.

The receptionist smiled at her and indicated a conference room to the left of the desk. Ava went in and waited. The long mahogany table was cold and bare except for a large vase of fresh flowers.

A man strode into another room, carrying a stack of papers. "Hello, I'm Clive Anderson. We spoke the other day. He held out a hand. When he saw Ava's attire, he added, "I'm sorry about your loss."

"Thank you," Ava said, shaking his hand and then sitting down again. No smiles for anyone today.

"Is your head okay now?" He asked.

"Yes, fine." The question caught Ava off guard.

"Are you sure you are okay? I heard you were having memory problems."

"No." Ava shook her head. "No problems."

"So, the will has gone missing. You'd be surprised how often that happens here, especially in cases where the signatory is elderly. We do have to go through some formalities before I can give you a copy of the papers. Do you have an ID?"

Ava handed him the card and waited. She could feel her nerves humming; she rarely had openly defied her mother in this way. However, the recent discoveries made her realise that their relationship was long over. She would need to do what she had to so she could move on with her life.

"Same name and same surname. Very good. And you said that you spoke to one of the witnesses."

"Yes, Mrs. Horridge. She lives in our neighbourhood and was one of my teachers when I went to secondary school."

"Well, that works out well. It all checks out. I had a copy of the document made before you came in. Your account was so specific that I suspected it would all be in order." The solicitor stood and handed her a stapled set of papers. "Be sure to put this copy in a safe place," he said with a laugh. "If you'd like, I can file the will with the probate courts. That should get the ball rolling for you, even though it can take time to process the will through probate. Would you like that?"

She stood and smiled, the first of the meeting. "Yes, please. That would be incredibly helpful. Thank you very much."

Ava drove around the corner and parked in a quiet neighbourhood. She couldn't wait to get home to read her grandfather's wishes. She pulled the papers from her bag and began to read.

The will had been written last year. She began to read the will. The text sounded like the words of her grandfather. The document was clear and concise, without any comments on the family.

He had given one hundred thousand pounds to each of his grandchildren. Ava raised her eyebrow and reread it. Yes, she and Luke were both given a substantial amount of money. After a few bequests to other people that she did not recognise, the remaining funds and the home were given to Donna and Vicki.

Ava had no idea of how much the entire estate was, but certainly, her mother and aunt couldn't begrudge her own children's money of their own. What did they have in mind?

The idea came to her mind. What if the women were keeping Ava and Luke under their thumb? If they controlled all the assets, then they would be able to manipulate the younger ones with funds or the threat of losing those funds. This would not be a matter of greed, but it would be a matter of power.

Ava knew what the power was needed for: both children were having flashbacks that could lead to the recognition of Donna's role in the abuse. Ava wasn't sure if her mother had participated in the abuse or merely covered it up for her father and the others. In either case, she had traumatised an unknown number of children over the years and then helped her father hide it. Perhaps their grandfather had been talking about confessing his sins. He'd always had a religious streak, but perhaps he had felt it time to admit to these crimes. Ava would have to learn more about the will and why it was being suppressed.

The will had been signed by Mrs. Horridge, as the teacher had told her – and Alfred Cook. Ava's blood froze as she read the name of the other owner of the Queen's Head. Cook was alive and still in York.

The information filled her with hope that she could find out more about what had happened – and nausea that this abuser was still alive and able to conduct business. Was he still involved in the child abuse operation? Ava felt a need to find out if that was true. She couldn't let other children go through the same pain she had felt through this.

Chapter 24

Ava talked to George about what she'd learned. He added a few points, but he hadn't been able to persuade her that her plan was not in her best interests.

"I'm going to talk to the police," Ava said with certainty. She'd decided on the way home from the law firm. The police would have to take this seriously and arrest Alfred Cook for his crimes.

"Ava, trust me. I have years of experience in this matter. If the police do take up the case, they're going to want more than you're able to give. They'll want names, dates, and places, and your flashbacks are not sufficient. By your own admission, they're fuzzy and incomplete. Even if they do arrest Cook, you'd have to testify in court. Sex cases are always the hardest on those who were abused. It's why so many people get away with the abuse."

"I still have to try," Ava replied, not budging in her convictions.

"You can, but you'll need to be prepared for the likely outcome. The police will decline to investigate. Either because the statutes of limitation have been reached or because there is not enough evidence to try the case. Either way, you won't get to court, and you'll be in the same place you are now."

"And if I found more people who had suffered the same thing?" Ava said.

"Then you could go to the police at that point. I don't want you to get upset when the police ignore you."

Ava nodded her head, but she was still adamant that she

would see the police. She still had a card up her sleeve.

The York Police Station was only a few blocks from George's flat, so Ava decided to walk there. She was nervous about the discussion and its outcome. While she had stood her ground when talking with George, she'd also taken his words to heart and feared that he was correct.

Thinking about discussing the abuse in the witness box terrified her. She would be asked hundreds of questions, but right now, she couldn't recall the adults who had abused the children. More children would help her put together the pieces.

Luke could not be relied upon. Ava felt that her mother had somehow managed to make Luke see her point of view. His one-time discussion of the flashbacks would be denied on the stand.

When she entered the building, the signs pointed Ava to a woman sitting at the reception desk. The officer looked up and asked how she could help.

"I'm here to report a crime," Ava said. For some reason, her voice had gone soft to where it was almost a whisper. Ava felt as though she was already being judged for reporting this.

"What type of crime?" The officer gave her a sympathetic smile. "I need to know to get the right person to talk to you."

Ava nodded. "Child abuse," she said, looking around to ensure no one had heard her.

The woman nodded and picked up the phone.

A few minutes later, a tall man stepped out of a room in the back of the building and approached Ava.

"What can I do for you? I understand you're here to report a crime?" He looked like he could solve anything. He had a muscled frame but was on the thin side, with short brown hair and round glasses that sat on his nose. He motioned Ava back toward the room where he came from.

Once they were in the small room with two chairs, rather

obvious video equipment, notepads, and pens, he pulled out a seat for her.

"It's best if you just start at the beginning. What happened?"

Ava told her story from the flashbacks to her brother's suicide attempt and her own flashbacks. She felt spent by the time she finished. The detective had taken notes while she spoke, but he never interrupted her. She was grateful for that, not knowing if she could have continued once she stopped.

"Well" the detective started, "I appreciate you telling me all this, but I'm not sure there's much we can do with the material you've given us. First, this appears to have happened twenty to twenty-five years ago. Given that we don't have a clear date, I would expect that a judge would rule against this moving forward. There's a time limit on how long someone has to report a crime, and this is past that limit."

"But," Ava started.

The detective held up his hand. "We're very aware that many victims don't recover their memories for decades, and they're children at the time, who would not be believed if the crimes were reported when they were young. It's a terrible thing, and I hate it, but I can't change the law."

"That's not right." Ava felt sick to her stomach now that the man had said it. She thought she would be ready for the restrictions, but the reality of the situation hurt.

"Well, add to that the fact that your grandfather is dead. Providing that he was the abuser, we don't prosecute dead people. Their crime dies with their death—even if they leave injured and hurt people in their wake. It's just the way that the system works."

"But there are others," Ava began, but then she stopped. She'd never met Alfred Cook. She didn't know what he looked like or if he'd even been in her flashbacks of that time. She had no proof whatsoever that he was involved — except for his name on the Queen's Head documents. Everything else was sheer speculation.

"Well, if you have nothing else, I'm very sorry. I wish I had better news." The man stood up and headed for the door.

"Wait, I do have another crime."

The man looked at Ava and then sat back down. "Is this another case of abuse?"

Ava shook her head. "No, attempted murder."

She started without invitation and told the whole story of being poisoned by arsenic and how her mother had been behind the attempt to kill her daughter.

"So, you do have hospital records for this case?" he said, writing down notes as he spoke.

"Yes, the doctor could easily show that I'd had multiple doses of arsenic."

"This is more likely to go to the courts," he said. The detective looked at her again.

" In the discussion we just had, you didn't indicate how the arsenic was introduced into your system. Can you be more specific about that?"

Ava took a deep breath. She was not going to get this arrest either. "I don't know. It had to be during the evening meal, but as far as I can tell, Donna gave us all the same food."

The man looked down for a minute and then returned his eyes to her face. "Without more information on how you were poisoned, the defense would argue that anyone at the meal could have committed the crime."

"But I was poisoned," Ava said, trying to convince the man of what she already knew.

The detective looked at her and gave her a wan smile. "I typically work sex crimes, which is why they brought me here. I don't usually work attempted murders. I can tell you that my mentor who worked several murders always said, 'With a case of poisoning, there is always a woman and a situation of coercive control.' Does that sound like your mother?"

Ava nodded. She wasn't going to get any help from the police on this matter. She would have to move forward and solve this on her own. The idea was daunting, but she had no other choice. Ava refused to let her mother win after all she'd been through.

Chapter 25

Ava knew her first step would be to find Alfred Cook. The repulsive man who had been in business with her grandfather was still alive—the only person to manage that feat—and he would have to tell her what had happened in the cellar.

If she found him, then perhaps the case could go on. She would have a living perpetrator who could be jailed for his sex crimes.

Of course, having such a common name, she would need to go back to making phone calls and see if she could find out if he was still alive and where he lived. Ava was by no means an investigator, and she hoped that some simple search would locate the man. She hated the idea that everyone who had been involved with this had passed away, leaving her and Luke with memories that would never go away.

Ava began with the local obituaries. After all, her own grandfather had been alive a year ago. She found it gruesome to look through the web pages of people who had passed away, but she couldn't think of another way to learn this information. As she'd been told by the police, she was on her own.

Other than feeling depressed that so many people grieved for the ones they'd lost, she came away with nothing. Ava realised that at one point, she, too, had felt sorrow for her grandfather's death, but now she was angry and bitter. She knew those feelings would ease—just as the feelings of those who grieved for the loss of someone.

Having done that, she started the phone marathon again.

Beginning with the first names of A since they were all Cooks, she began to make calls. She didn't find any Alfreds, so everyone was a possibility here.

She had made it about halfway through the list when she got her first lead. "Hello, is Alfred Cook there?" she asked, feeling like a robot on a loop.

"No, he's not," the voice answered.

It took Ava a second to realise that the woman had not said that there was no one by that name. This person was not at home.

"When do you expect him back?" Ava asked, feeling nervous and excited. She might finally get some answers and some closure to this horrible situation.

"When the doctors let him out—if they let him out—he's at York General Hospital now." The woman did not sound overly upset, so Ava continued her questions. Perhaps the older man was not very ill.

"I'm sorry to hear that," Ava said. She was sorry because she wanted Alfred Cook to be healthy when she confronted him. So much relied on him.

"He's getting up there, you know?" the woman said.

Ava said her goodbyes and made plans to confront Alfred Cook. It would be awkward to ask him questions there, but since she was technically an "old friend" of the family, she could pretend to be there as a concerned visitor.

Ava thought about getting a new outfit for the visit. None of the clothes she'd brought with her seemed appropriate for a hospital, though she couldn't think of any clothing that matched this occasion. She was going to the hospital to confront a man about what happened in the cellar.

George was still with patients, and she decided not to wait to tell him what she'd uncovered. After the meeting with the police, who had offered her no hope—and no action, she felt the need to go and confront this man, the abuser who had made money from her pain.

Ava was still trying to decide how to start the conversation when she got to the hospital. The information desk was empty, so she asked a nurse to help her. The woman pointed her to a lift and told her cardiac patients were on the eighth floor.

She found the room easily. However, the person who answered the phone was overly optimistic. The patients on this floor looked like they had little time left.

Fortunately, each room in this wing was for a single patient. Ava wondered how she would have handled the accusations if there had been another witness to the confrontation.

She walked into the room, and the old man lifted his head up. "Well, well, if it isn't little Miss Ava. I'd have recognised you anywhere." However, Ava did not recognise the man with his thin hair and drooping eyelids. She could see little beneath his neck with the sheets and blankets covering him.

The voice, though, brought back a million images in her mind, but she pushed them down for the moment. She had no time to deal with this side of the abuse. That could come later. Now she wanted information.

"I'm in town, and I wanted to pay my respects," she said, starting softer than she'd planned. Ava thought a slow, conciliatory attitude would get her more answers than direct accusations.

He laughed. "That'll be the day. More'n likely you came to see if I was dead yet. Well, I'm still here."

"You knew that my grandfather passed away? I came back for the funeral." Ava shuffled her feet back and forth, feeling the grinding tension in her own body. She remembered this man. Ava had hated him with a passion when she'd been younger. She hadn't understood then what was behind these emotions as a girl. Now she knew.

"I knew it. The old bastard outlived most of his friends. It was time for him to go." He leaned forward and coughed to punctuate his sentence. "Many people there?"

"Not many. He'd been sick for years, so he lost track of most people he knew."

"That's not the only reason," the man said, coughing again as he finished his sentence.

Ava was puzzled. She thought that the two men had been business partners and friends. Cook did not sound like he would miss her grandfather at all. Had they had a falling out? Had something caused them to dissolve the partnership and go their own ways? That would explain why the pub had been sold to another business, a more legitimate place to meet.

"That's not very nice to say about the dead," Ava said, trying her best to keep a poker face—expressing no emotion at all. She'd learned to do that at home.

"Like you'll be sorry to see me go," Cook said with a barking laugh that made him cough again. He pressed a hand against his heart—as if he was praying. Ava wondered if his own tension was affecting him, too.

"I did take the trouble of looking you up," Ava said. "I spoke to someone at the house who told me you were here."

The man grunted but didn't speak. Ava had hoped for a name or a relationship between the person on the phone and Cook. She thought that if Ava had been abused by her own grandfather, the person on the phone might have been abused as well. She had given up on Luke as a witness to what they'd done. However, Ava still wanted some sort of verification, and another person could say, "Yes, this has happened."

"I wanted to talk to you about the Queen's Head," Ava said. The coughs and noises seemed to stop until it was only the sound of the machines hooked up to Cook and his breathing.

"What is that—a film?" he asked. He chuckled to himself,

and Cook began to cough again. "A documentary on all the bad things your family did in York? That'd be a long film for sure."

Ava's fists clenched at the denial. She knew it would be hard to get him to confess, but at the same time, he was likely on his deathbed. This floor of the hospital was a hospice wing, where people were made comfortable before they died. Now was the time, if ever, to make a confession. Did Cook really plan to go to the grave with this crime on his mind? If so, then Ava was sunk.

"I'm talking about the pub you and my grandfather owned." Ava walked over to the tray above his bed and pushed the corporate documentation to show their "business."

Cook leaned forward, snatched the papers, and ripped them into pieces. "That's what I think of your papers." Ava was surprised that he had that much energy in him.

"I have more," Ava said. "I'm not stupid enough to give you my only copy. I have plenty of them for everyone. Do you want your family to get copies of this?"

"You wouldn't dare. None of you are strong enough to pull off that stunt." Cook sat up fully now and stared at her. "You'll be crying before you leave here because I will not confess to your little conspiracy theory. Then what?"

Ava was not going to give in, that was certain. Now, she added to the list of things she wanted to walk away with. "I can do this without you, but I'd hate to see the last months of your life in a jail cell, trying to defend yourself over these charges. All that money you made will be used up in the trial, and then what? Your family will be broke. You won't be able to leave them anything. Is that what you want?"

Cook coughed and tried to speak, but nothing came out.

Ava slapped down another paper. "You were still in cahoots with my grandfather at the end of his life. Your name is on his will. You were a witness along with Mrs. Horridge."

The reaction on his face made Ava see that she should have started with the will. His face grew white, and his knuckles were whiter as he clutched the edge of the bed sheet. "I don't know anything about that."

"That's not what I was told by others. Committing a crime relies on no one knowing what's going on. With a will, it's the opposite. You need a solicitor and two witnesses. I can get others to make your version look like the lies they are."

"I have nothing to say," the man said. There was no cough now, but he was still clearly frightened.

Ava stopped goading him for a moment. She had become lost in thought regarding the will. What did he know that he was so frightened of? Had Donna and Vicki paid him off to get this silence?

Ava suggested that to him now. He lost the frightened look he had, but the expression was replaced by a curious look that Ava couldn't place. His brows were furrowed, and his eyes were nearly closed. Was he worried—but about what? She had difficulty reading the look of a man she hadn't seen in over twenty years.

This man was hiding more than one lie. Ava felt frustrated that she had so little time to determine what they were, yet each was so important. She thought she only had a fraction of the pieces she needed for this puzzle.

"Look, I'm not trying to get you in trouble for the will. I know what happened, but I need to hear you say it. Maybe all that money should go to the children who were abused."

"And who is that? Twenty-five years it's been since you were a kid, and no one has said a peep about any form of abuse. And the Queen's Head—or whatever you called it—is not heard of in the news either. It would be a big story if that happened."

Ava nodded. "It certainly would be a big news story. I was

giving you a chance, but if you don't confess, I'll have to take this to the news myself. That would not be good for your health."

"Nothing can help my health now," Alfred Cook said. "I'm beyond hope."

"All the more reason to tell me what happened, your perspective," Ava said. She could feel the tension in her. Now, she had a deadline with Alfred Cook. Until this point, Ava could work at her own place as she felt it, but now she didn't have a choice. At some point soon, he would die, and his stories would turn to dust, just as he did.

"You wearing a wire?" he asked. "Better show me."

Ava looked at him with disgust. "You just want me to undress," she said. "I think you've seen enough of me." She felt a shiver of repulsion. This man had been her abuser, and he'd felt no compunction over what he'd done. She wondered—and decided—that her grandfather had been the same way, unrepentant until the last moment of his criminal life. Ava could at least rest easy with the knowledge that both men would be dead soon—and the world would have two fewer evil men on this planet.

He laughed until he began to choke again. "You don't know anything about what happened. It's clear. Did all that wipe out your memories?" He stared at her, and Ava stood there without answering. "You don't know, do you? No wonder you're missing the facts of that story. I'll be damned. You have nothing on us. You can't go to the police with a missing memory. They'll laugh you out of there, just like I'm doing to you. Must be frustrating, right?"

"It's coming back more and more. And I have other people who have remembered the same abuse, the same cellar, the same disgusting people who did this."

"Luke, don't count. He'd never get up in front of a jury and betray his mother. She's got him around her finger."

"I didn't say 'Luke.' Ava said. "I used the word others. You can go down with the ship if you want, but the end of this is coming soon. I'll see to it."

Alfred Cook tried to sit up, but the effort was too much for him. He began to cough again, but now the sound did not stop. He began to spit up something into a cloth, and he punched the button for medical help.

Ava decided that now was the time to leave, so she went in the opposite direction from the nurses' station. She could hear the nurse approach as she left the hallway.

While Ava had struck out with Alfred Cook, she had yet to try the woman who had answered his phone. When she returned to the flat, Ava picked up her phone and dialed the number that had rewarded her with Cook's location.

After five rings, the same woman answered the phone, which took Ava by surprise. "Hello, I called earlier. My name is Ava Hedges," she started.

The woman began to laugh. "I know that name all too well. And what did you want with my grandfather? Probably the same things that everyone else who calls him these days. Money, confession, apologies. Let me guess. You didn't get a single one of those things."

Ava winced at the woman's accurate statements. Others had approached Cook to confront him about the abuse ring. Was this woman just cynical, or was she supporting the abuser?

"Actually, I wanted to talk to you. I've filed charges against Alfred Cook for his abuse of children two decades ago."

The woman's laugh stopped. "And they turned you away. I told you that the statute of limitations has expired, meaning he can't be prosecuted for his crimes." Her voice was quiet, almost a somber tone now.

"Exactly. Did you do the same thing?" Ava asked.

"Not me. I'm still alive. But others have tried."

"And they've been killed—or injured for doing so?"

"Not really. A few took their own lives, but mostly, they just gave up, which is just as bad in my book. Then, I decided that I was not going to do anything about it either. It happened, and now we have to live with it. That's all I have to say to you. Move on and get over it."

Before Ava could speak again, the phone had disconnected.

Chapter 26

When Ava finished the phone call, she was more determined than ever to investigate this matter.

One person who had been an adult during the time of the abuse was her father, who had been gone for years. Ava wanted to know now if he had recognised what had gone on in the cellar and if he'd left because of it. She didn't give him much credit for leaving his two children there to suffer, but she could understand why he couldn't stand by and watch that happen. Ava realised that she blamed her mother most of all. How could she have ignored what was happening? She had to know.

However, her search ended abruptly. There was no sign of an Oliver Hedges anywhere in the York area. Now she wondered how far her father had gone to escape Donna. Her bitterness and the abuse had likely made him want to move as far as possible.

She was trying to determine her next step when George came home. He gave her a big smile and a kiss, then he shut the door and sat down on the sofa. "What have you been up to today?" he asked. "Work was busy. There were three new intakes and an issue with an existing patient." He rested his head on the back of the sofa and looked up.

When he realised that Ava had not answered, he sat up again.

Ava had already decided that she would be honest with George. The way her mother behaved would not be the way that her children acted. She wanted to have a working relationship with George, which meant telling the truth.

"I went and talked to the police today," Ava started. She went through the interview with the detective and his feeling that the case would never be brought to court. Then she started on her quest for Alfred Cook and how she had found him in the hospital.

"How did that go?" George asked. He was clearly listening to her every word.

"Not well. He refused to admit anything. He just laughed a lot—and coughed. I talked to someone else at his house, a granddaughter, I think, who vaguely admitted that she was an abuse victim, but she told me to get over it."

"That's to be expected. An abuser is not likely to have a change of heart and confess. In my profession, most people see themselves as good people. They'll tell you that at length. They're good, but people just don't understand them. I see so many people who want to make you see their perspective, no matter how skewed it is."

Ava looked at him. "And you're telling me that Alfred Cook sees himself as a good person?" Ava never thought of those men as anything other than evil. How could they not see that as well?

"Yes, it's part of their self-identity, and it's nearly impossible to have them change their personal view." George smiled. "It keeps me employed."

Ava just shook her head. "I can't believe that."

"Do you think that your mother thinks she's a bad mother? She poisoned you, but if you asked, she would tell you that she's always been a loving, caring mother. No one says I'm a bad person. I'd be shocked if any of the people involved with this abuse ring would tell you that."

Ava rubbed her temples. This made no sense. These people had done horrendous things to young children, and yet they would see themselves as "good people." She was baffled at the human mind and spirit.

" What's next?" George asked. "Are you going to work on your own flashbacks or talk to Luke or something else?"

Ava could tell that George wanted her to work on her own mental health. When he made multi-part suggestions, he always listed his preference first. Ava had already begun to see the quirks of the man she was living with, and she had to admit that she enjoyed staying here. The thought of going back to her mother's house was more than she could handle, especially now that she suspected her mother of being complicit in the abuse ring.

She just wished she could understand what had happened. She had fragments and pieces, but no complete puzzle. There were still too many holes.

Ava told George, "I'm looking for my father. He seems to be a key piece of this puzzle, and he is missing. He might be able to explain things to me."

George's lips went into a straight line, and then he took a deep breath. "Are you sure that's a good idea?" he asked. "He could be a disappointment to you, and I'm just thinking that you've been through a lot lately. I would hate to see you get another blow from your family in terms of what they've done."

Ava thought about it for a second, but she still wanted to know what had happened to her father. Why had he left? What were the reasons? "Yes, I'm pretty sure I can handle whatever I learn about him. I don't feel like he was a member of that abuse group."

George nodded. "You're the best judge of your situation. I'm just a guide." He smiled.

"I looked in the sites for local phone numbers for Oliver Hedges, and I'm not finding anything. Do you have suggestions on searches?"

"Let's start with what you remember. Do you remember

him leaving? I recall that you mentioned he said goodbye to you and Luke. Is that right?"

Ava nodded. "He pulled us aside and told us he couldn't stay any longer. But he would be back for us."

"In those words?" George asked.

Ava tried to remember the exact wording from that moment in time, but the incident had become a series of amber moments. "I'm not sure. Maybe I hoped that he would come back for us?"

"But he told you that he was leaving. Okay, so did he tell you anything about where he was going?

Ava bit her lip as she tried to recall. "I don't think so."

"And did he tell you why he was leaving?" George was making some notes on a discarded notepad. "What his motivation was?"

"No, but would you tell that to a ten-year-old?" she asked.

George sighed and sat back. "I don't know because we don't know the circumstances. Would he have left you if he knew you were being abused? At the very least, he would be back as soon as he could to rescue you. And if he didn't know, what was his motivation for leaving?"

Ava shrugged. "I don't know. Our family was never easy to get along with. There could have been a number of reasons. The question I have is: what happened to him in the past twenty years? Where is he now?"

"Well, you were uncertain about their divorce and his part of the estate. I was thinking that we could start with some of the local records and see what we could find out?"

Ava took her phone and started scrolling through the records she could find. She stopped and stared at the one entry. "Uh, George, you might want to look at this."

She numbly handed her phone to George, who read the transcript and then handed it back to her.

"What the hell is this?" she asked. "Donna filed a petition to have my father declared dead. She never said a word about this. I was still at home, and she did this behind our backs."

"Do you think that Luke knew?" George asked.

"I'm not sure why he would. He was younger than me, and I would have been about eighteen."

" She did this behind your back and then let you believe that your father was still alive. That gave you hope for a reconciliation when none was possible."

Ava stared at the screen again. "I don't have the exact dates, but it seems she didn't waste any time. It was about seven years after he left. Do you think she knew that he wouldn't be returning? I mean, she could have killed him. We know she poisoned me, and we think she might have poisoned my grandfather—what's one more?"

"That's quite a stretch," George said. "I mean, it's possible, but we've just made your mother into a serial killer. That's a big step up from greedy and Factitious disorder."

"If we could get a copy of the court transcript, we might be able to learn more. Maybe Donna provided some details that he was dead, or maybe she said something that could be considered incriminating."

"That's possible but unlikely. However, it might be able to give you more details about what happened. It definitely sounds like your mother has not been honest with you."

Ava snorted, which expressed her opinion of her mother. Donna had never been honest with her, and now she lied about her father and his disappearance. "I'm not finding any information about her divorce. It sounds like she and my father didn't get a divorce, then after the allotted time, she went to court and had him declared dead—so the estate would be hers without any claim by my father. Even back then, she was thinking about the money."

"Do you think that the money came from your grandfather's," George cleared his throat. "endeavors?"

Ava gave him a little smile. He dealt with the worst of humanity at times, but he still felt a need to paint over the ugliness. He used a much kinder word for her grandfather than she would have chosen. "Probably. My father was a postmaster, and Donna didn't work to my knowledge. I seem to recall that she got payments from her father at times, which makes me think that she was involved in the abuse ring."

" Now what?" George asked. He seemed to have had enough of this discussion and wanted a more pleasant topic.

Ava was happy to appease him. She had spent the day looking into her past, and she could use a nice break. She got up and made them both some tea.

When she returned, George was looking through her notes. "I hope you don't mind. I was just being curious about the matter. I hoped I would get a flash of inspiration."

"Anything come to mind?" she asked.

"It would need to be a big mind. I'm afraid I don't have that. Something really big." George stopped and stared at the wall for a few seconds.

"Okay, well, something is happening. What is it?"

"We should start looking for where his body could have been put. It hasn't been found in twenty-plus years, and it has to be somewhere. Perhaps we need to look around."

Ava made a face because she saw the obvious answer as well. "The cellar. I have to return to that cellar and see if we can find anything."

Chapter 27

Ava shot up in bed and looked around. Her heart raced, and her breathing came in gasps. She'd had another flashback, the second one tonight. Ava thought—no, hoped—that these were only coming from her work trying to learn more about her family. She couldn't bear it if they were permanent.

Tonight's had been the worst so far. The first one started with the mysterious hand tugging her down the stairs to the cellar and leaving her there. The faceless people surrounded her, and the first one made their move.

Ava had screamed when the first hand touched her. She was powerless to escape the unwanted caress. It repulsed her, and no amount of struggling stopped the abuse. How could anyone find that attractive?

She had woken up around 11 p.m. with that sense of upset stomach and anxiety. George had slept through it, and she was grateful. Ava had no desire to continue the discussions about her past. She wished she could go back to the days when this was all stuffed away in the cubby of her mind. These memories were too horrible to relive regularly.

The second one had been more vivid, if that was possible. She had been dragged down the stairs again, but this time, she saw the faces of the other children who were also there. Ava felt an overwhelming guilt that she could not save these children, the ones who had suffered like her. However, because they were so young, she doubted she could find any of them now.

In one corner, she saw Luke with another faceless adult. Ava tried to call for him, but her voice was silent. Nothing came out. Since he didn't see her, he made no move to look at her.

He sat there and stared at a shelf in the cellar. It was almost like he was a statue, frozen and emotionless. Two people approached him, and Luke still made no move. However, Ava knew better. After all, Luke had tried to kill himself after experiencing one of those flashbacks. That is not the reaction of someone who has things under control.

Now, she sat up in bed, panicking about the likely upcoming flashbacks. How much longer would these last?

She would need to ask George if there were treatments to make them stop.

Quietly, she slipped out of bed, grabbing her laptop on the way out. Ava had decided to be productive in the wee hours. Maybe she could learn more about Alfred Cook and his life since the man had made it clear that he would tell her nothing.

Ava went to an ancestry website and created an account. She had decided to start with a family tree for the Cooks. She had no idea if there was a Mrs. Cook, children, or grandchildren. If they existed, perhaps the older generation would have participated in the cellar's horrendous acts. If there was a younger generation, Ava was sure that they had not escaped the abuse.

She quickly found records about the man; yes, he'd been married. However, the wife had passed away twenty years ago. Ava wondered how the woman had died and if it might have been a suicide when or if she'd learned of her husband's activities. She couldn't determine the timeline of those events.

They had one child, a girl named Lucy.

For obvious reasons, she couldn't call at this time of night, but she checked the directory online. She couldn't find a single reference for a Lucy Cook. The ancestry site did not show that Lucy had married anyone, so presumably, her last name would not have changed. Because it was such a common name, Ava was certain that many women were named Lucy Cook. Her quest would be harder. The site gave her no indications of what had happened to the girl. Maybe she'd died, but then she'd quickly found the death certificate of the wife.

Growing frustrated with the lack of information, Ava quickly created a family tree for her own family. This tree became full of information, in part because she knew the answers to all of the questions about births and deaths.

Her mother's name popped up as a possible familial match, and Ava clicked the X so that it did not inform her mother that she was online. No matter what the reason for being here, Donna would make the new account a reflection of her in some way.

She added her father and Luke to the chart, and her grandfather came next. Interestingly, the site already had information about his death, and Ava added that to the chart as well.

She saw no signs of Vicki in the family tree, but that was fine with Ava. She didn't want to think about her anyway. She was twice as bad as her mother. Donna's account did show Vicki as a sibling, but it appeared that Donna had used a manual input of details rather than the documents often used to tie family members together.

Having done all that, she began to try to find more information on her father—post-departure. There was nothing. No marriages, divorces, no other children, and no markers of death. It was just like he had disappeared.

This new data made Ava more suspicious. Perhaps Donna had done away with him. The court-ordered declaration of death meant more money for her mother. Ava felt a wave of sadness that she was investigating her mother as a possible murderer.

Running out of clues to her questions, Ava decided to go

back to sleep. She shut the laptop and headed back to the bedroom.

When she woke the next day, George was making tea in the kitchen. She could hear the now familiar sounds of his morning ritual. He hadn't needed to get up at his normal time; he had called in and planned so that he could go to the cellar with Ava.

Ava was a little uncertain of his company. On the one hand, it was sweet and supportive, which she could use. However, she was concerned that the growing emotions she had from the flashbacks and memories would lead her to cry or get angry while they were in that space. She didn't want George to see her in that shape.

She went to the loo and splashed water across her face. Ava thought she looked pale, but who could blame her after the night she had? Using old-school methods, she pinched her cheeks to make them rosy, and she put a soft rose lipstick across the thin-lined lips. Ava assessed herself and thought that she would have to do.

Ava and George had developed a plan by the time they reached the Prince Gentleman's Pub. George would sit at the bar, order a drink for the two of them, and then Ava would sneak down to the cellar and look for anything that might indicate a burial there. If the bartender were the same one who had caught her in the cellar on her last visit, then they would cancel the search.

The pub was not empty but far from full, and Ava was concerned that her absence would be noticed far earlier than if the bar was packed. As planned, George ordered two drinks. Ava took a sip of her liquid courage and then went off to the loo, which was next door to the cellar entrance. She took one look back, and George gave her a thumbs up.

Fortunately, the door didn't squeak, and it was still unlocked, even after her last foray into the lower levels. She had a torch this time around, so she didn't need any additional light. It would prove less noticeable if someone opened the door.

Once she was down the stairs, Ava began to search the corners and nooks of the cellar, hoping to see any signs of an indentation in the dirt floor or any marks that showed her that the floor had been adjusted in any way. The spaces near the wall were lined with shelves, and there was no way that she could move them—there was no way that George or all her friends could. So, she skipped those, thinking that too many people would have spread the details of a death before this.

The rest was floor space in the middle of the cellar. Ava doubted that the space could have been used to bury someone. The abuser met two to three times a week.

Ava paused, wondering how she knew this. Had she just imagined that, or had that information come to her in one of the flashbacks?

Standing there, she began to see another image from the past. She swallowed hard. In previous memories, she had only seen but never heard the voices. Today—in the place where all that pain had occurred—she started to hear the voices. Little children and adults, too. Ava recalled that Luke had told her that he had begun to experience other senses in his flashbacks, especially the sense of smell. That was how she had first wondered about a pub when he smelled the alcohol in the room.

She heard the children crying, most of them between eight and thirteen. Ava again didn't know how she knew that, but she knew it as well as her own name. These were primary school children. What had these people been doing?

She heard the laughter of the adults, and Ava felt another rumbling in her stomach, and she feared that she would get sick again, as she had last time.

Fortunately, her concentration was broken by the sound of her mobile. George had sent her a message: "The bartender is trying to find a woman to go into the loo to look for you. He's concerned you're not well."

Ava pushed the phone back into her pocket and hurried up the stairs. She managed to get into the loo seconds before a tall blonde came into the room. "You Ava?" the woman asked in a deep voice.

Ava nodded and wiped her mouth as if she'd vomited. "Yeah, feeling a little sick. Don't tell the boyfriend – or that bartender either—I think I might be pregnant." She had come up with the lie, thinking that no one would want to spoil the news by telling people about it.

However, Ava hadn't planned on the several-minute lecture on what to do and what not to do. By the time she left the loo, she was ready to buy nappies.

George raised an eyebrow, and Ava gave him a quick thumbs down. He nodded.

They left the pub and walked down the street. Ava was ready to go back to George's flat and spend the rest of the day, but George had other plans. He dialed a number and asked for Donna.

He made a few noises and then rang off.

Ava's mouth felt like it had hit the floor. What was he doing calling her mother?

"Donna's not home, and Luke is going out. We could visit the house if you want." George looked proud as if he had found the clue that solved the case. Only he hadn't.

"If we're going someplace, let's go to my grandfather's house. It's close to the other house, and it's less likely to have people wandering around. We could get in and out in no time."

George shrugged and held the car door open. "It's your choice, darling."

Ava made George drive around the block three times to ensure that no one was at her grandfather's house and no one was at her childhood home. They parked two blocks away and walked to the empty house.

Her grandfather had always kept a key under a large rock in the front garden, and Donna had not changed that tradition. Ava unlocked the front door and slid the key back where it had been. They entered the house quietly and waited for any sound. They heard none.

"Where's the cellar in this place?" George asked, looking at the number of doors in the hallway. "This place is huge."

Ava took his hand and led him down the hallway to the third door on the left. "This is it," she announced, opening the door. No one was there, and Ava breathed a lungful of relief.

They went down the stairs and turned on the light. The space had not changed at all. The boxes were all over, and some of the same type of shelves sat around the outside of the room. That resemblance only made her realise how much the two places had in common.

George had taken the torch and began to look around the various edges of the room. There wasn't much to see as the shelves and boxes rested on the ground. The boxes were far too heavy for George alone, and Ava deduced that from the grunting he did as he tried to carry them.

"Want some help on that?" she asked. She did a mock flex to show her biceps.

He laughed. "Sure, I can use all the help I can get." George moved over so that she could get in beside him.

They moved simultaneously and settled the box off to one side. George indicated the next box, and again, they moved it off to the free space on the adjoining wall. Ava was feeling the ache of her muscles from moving heavy loads. She might have spoken too soon in her jest to George.

The third box was heavier, and combined with the previous work, Ava could feel the box slipping from her hands as they started to move it.

The box hit the dirt floor, and the side of the box split open. A landslide of photos and nick-knacks fell out of the box. Ava didn't recognise the various keepsakes, but the photos intrigued her.

Donna didn't keep any images. She said that she wanted to look ahead and never look behind. Ava had always thought it peculiar, but now she was seeing all of the photos from their childhood and times earlier than that.

George stopped trying to push the box and came over to see what Ava was pulling out of the box. "I appreciate you lightening my load, but one photo at a time seems rather slow, don't you think?"

She ignored his attempt at humor and pulled out two more photos. One was Luke and herself, and Ava set that aside.

"Is that you?" George asked, picking up the photo.

She nodded. "I can't believe I was ever that young."

Ava threw down four more images into another pile.

"Is that you, too?" George asked.

Ava smacked his arm lightly. "Don't even say that in jest. No, not at all. That's Vicki."

George looked at the photo more closely. Ava pointed a finger at the photo. "See, she has dark eyes. People's eyes don't change from dark to light. It doesn't happen that way."

She paused and started counting on her fingers. After a few minutes, she looked at George. "Did your college classes include genetics? Recessive and dominant genes, and all that stuff?"

George had a look on his face that was clearly confused. "Yeah, it's been a while, but I know the basics. What's up? Are you trying to get out of being a Hedges?"

Ava laughed. "Don't I wish. No, I wanted to know if two people with green eyes could have a child with brown eyes. That can't happen, can it?"

"Are you planning our children already?" he asked. George tried to play it off as a joke, which frustrated Ava. She wanted the answer now.

He must have sensed her anger. "It's all rather complicated. We used to think that there was only one gene for eye color, but it turns out there are more. You need a chart to figure out what the chances are for two green-eyed parents to have a brown-eyed baby. It's uncommonly rare, I mean like less than a percent, but it is possible. Can I ask why we're doing basic genetics in your grandfather's cellar?"

"My grandfather and his wife both had green eyes," Ava pulled a picture out of the mess and showed George her grandparents. "She died a long time ago. I was in primary school then. But I remember her eyes. They were beautiful."

"And your grandfather had them too?" George asked. Ava was certain that he hadn't figured out where she was going with this discussion.

"Yeah, he had deep green eyes, but he always wore sunglasses, even in the house. It was so common that they put the sunglasses on him at the funeral."

"Maybe he had an eye condition that made him wear glasses?" George suggested. "A lot of people have them as they get older."

"I think that his eye condition was that he had green eyes. People would be sure to ask him how Vicki got brown eyes if she was his daughter. And he wore dark glasses so people wouldn't be able to see his eyes."

"Wait a minute. Are you saying that your aunt is not a blood relative? How did she get to their house, then? It's not like people just drop off a kid to strangers."

"What if she wasn't a stranger? What if the other parents knew my grandfather? Say, maybe run a business with them?"

George ran a hand through his hair, giving him a cute air when a few curls fell over his eyes. "That's a huge jump of logic there, Ms. Holmes. You're saying that Vicki was the daughter of the Cooks. They gave her to your grandfather, and he raised her. She even has the family name. Why would they do all that?"

Then the realisation hit him, and his eyes widened. Ava could see his mind working as he saw what Ava had suspected.

"Would anyone do that? I mean, that's disgusting."

"At this point, I wouldn't be surprised by anything that happened here. This is a funhouse where everything is backward and upside down. Now, I need you to help me find a lockbox. If I remember correctly, it was about six inches by nine inches. It was a brassy color and had handles on both sides. If we can find that, we'll find some answers to the Vicki question." Ava could feel that George was skeptical, the entire thing was hard to believe, but he had accepted that the abuse and the poisoning were real. Anything else could be suspicious as well.

"Why would it be down here?" George asked. "It doesn't seem like the best place to keep important papers."

"I've seen a few photos in here that used to be upstairs in his bedroom. I believe Donna cleared out the bedroom and dumped it all down here. So, get looking!"

Three hours later, George found it—in the seventh box he rummaged through. It had been tucked in the corner of a packing box.

Of course, the box did not have a key, so Ava found a screwdriver and opened it. The box contained several papers dating back to the late 1900s. She dumped the contents on the floor and began to sort through them.

The review of the box went slowly. Ava didn't want to miss any document that might come in handy later. She found the documents regarding the court case where her father had been declared dead. She put those in her pocket as a remembrance of her father and a potential clue to his whereabouts.

She also found a copy of her grandfather's will, signed by Mrs. Horridge and Alfred Cook. It was much as what she'd been told. Each grandchild received a flat sum, and the two daughters, if Vicki was really a daughter, split the rest of the estate. Ava now wondered if Donna had plans to keep the entire thing for herself. If there were no will, it would go to the surviving next of kin. If Vicki weren't officially adopted, then she would not be the next of kin. Donna would have all the estate, every last penny of it.

One more piece of paper was of interest. Ava and George had not found any indication that Vicki had been adopted or even fostered by the Farley's. Ava located a piece of paper that allowed Arthur Farley to act as Vicki's temporary parent. The document had been signed by Alfred Cook, and Ava wondered what his wife had said about giving away their only daughter for the use of an abuser. The thought of what happened made her sick.

She explained all this to George, who nodded. The scheme made sense to them both. Donna was not above doing whatever it took to get the house and the money. After all, she'd tried to scare Ava with poison. What else would she do?

They decided to stop for the day and clean up the boxes. When they finished, it wasn't exactly as it had been. Still, unless Donna had been meticulous, which was nearly impossible, she'd never know they'd been through the belongings.

Chapter 28

After making multiple copies of the documents, Ava decided to visit Luke. Now that she had proof of the will and Donna's perfidy, she wanted to confront him, hoping that he would snap out of Donna's power over him. The idea that Donna would control him, after all the horrible things she'd done, appalled Ava, and she wanted to break that bond.

Ava had decided to go alone. She talked over the matter with George, who felt that Luke would be more open to discussing issues without a therapist present. After some thought, Ava agreed.

She went to the house, praying that Donna and Vicki would not be there. She needed the time to talk to Luke one-on-one.

With his first line, Ava knew that this would be an uphill battle.

"What are you doing here? Trying to convince me that I've made the wrong decisions in my life –or maybe you want to convince me to leave my mother. Is that it?" Luke had on an old T-shirt and tight jeans. Ava didn't want to know where he was going or what he was doing. It was too much for her to think that the abuse had caused her brother to behave like that.

"I did want to talk to you," Ava said. "There are some things that you need to see." She handed over the documents she'd found in her grandfather's cellar.

Luke took the papers, flipped through them, and then handed them to Ava again. "So, what does this mean?"

"Mum is cutting us out of the will," Ava said. "You could be free. You wouldn't have to do these things for money."

"Ava, this is nothing I don't know. I found this out months ago. I'm not stupid. She had the old will on the kitchen table— just out in the open. Mother has a lot of good qualities, but she's not subtle."

Ava was shocked. "You knew that she was stealing our money? How could you let her do that?"

He laughed. "I don't know how to manage large sums of money. The money that I have will be handled by Mum. She'll care for the estate and give me what I need."

She could not believe her ears. Their mother had never shown any signs of assisting her children. She had sold them to abusers for money and her own sick thrills. Ava could not believe that Luke would be that gullible.

Remembering what George had told her about the children who clung to their parents, no matter what. She had assumed that this would change when the children grew up, but apparently, that was not the case. Luke was still clutched to Donna as if she would do no harm. Ava knew better. Her mother was capable of anything.

Luke laughed again. "I know what's going on here. I choose to play my hand in a different way than you do. You want the nice doctor, and a good life. I'm happy with the life I have now. I get by."

"She won't leave you a penny," Ava said.

"I'll walk out of here alive," he said. "That's a damn lot better than the other option."

Ava didn't understand what he was talking about. Luke was the one who attempted to take his own life. No one had threatened him in any way—that she knew of.

Then it hit her. The same person who had poisoned Ava had also attempted to kill Luke as well. She wondered now if the amount of poison she'd given Luke was enough to kill him—or just enough to make sure he got the message about her intent. Cross Donna Hedges and die.

"Ah, I can see from your face that you've figured it out." Luke crossed his arms over his chest. "You see, I had an unfair advantage with the 'suicide' attempt." Luke made air quotes around the words. "I knew I hadn't done it."

"Then what happened?" Ava asked. She was shocked by how calm Luke was about the entire matter. Her own reaction to the poisoning was far worse than his. However, to be frank, she ended up in the same circumstances as Luke. They both knew that Donna had attempted to kill them, but nothing could be done about it.

"Those were an old bottle of pills. I thought I'd disposed of them ages ago, but I'm guessing that if I did, our mother found the bottle in the bin and saved it for an emergency. Donna didn't realise that I was content where I was. She thought that I would make a claim against the estate as soon as our grandfather had died. I'd taken photos of the pages of the will I found, and she felt threatened by that. Never push her into a corner; she'll fight hard."

Ava knew that. She was living with her boyfriend now and away from the family she thought she had.

"What would have happened if I hadn't found you?" Ava asked, wondering if he'd thought about the consequences of his game with their mother.

He shrugged. "I'm not sure. The pills were weak. They were years old and far past the expiration date. So, they might not have done the job. But you came along and called 999, so I didn't have to worry about that. You saved the day." His words sounded sincere, but the sneer on his face made her realise that he wasn't happy.

"But you said you wanted to live?" Ava asked. "Why are you behaving this way?"

He laughed. "You gave me no choice but to live. No one

asked me if I liked having these flashbacks and the way I feel about myself. No one questioned what it was like to be stuck in a home with someone who tried to kill you."

Ava started to cry. She hadn't meant to do that today, but Luke's story was heartbreaking, yet he seemed to go along with whatever Donna wanted. She couldn't grasp why anyone would do that—so she asked him.

"It's not that easy," Luke said. "I went through tons of therapy, literally weeks and months of daily talk sessions. The people who abused you can also be the people you want to emulate. They're the ones with power. You get the chance to mimic them, hoping that you'll be the one who has the power and the authority. I can see what I'm doing wrong, but I can't stop it. It's like I watch the action in a movie, and I can shout out for the character to be smarter, but they can't hear me. I can see what I'm doing, but I can't stop that from happening. The same way when I give in to what Donna wants, and I can't stop myself from doing it."

Ava hadn't experienced that kind of reaction to the abuse. Hers had come later, and perhaps that was part of it. Or she had built up better coping mechanisms since she was far from her family and the site of the abuse. No wonder Donna didn't like Ava. She couldn't control her daughter in the same way as her son. Ava represented a threat to her stolen estate and the house.

"Well, since we're telling each other the truth. I think Donna killed Dad." Ava said. The words sounded so awkward as she said them, like a melodrama.

Luke laughed. "No shit."

Ava couldn't believe her ears. "You knew that? Did she tell you?"

Luke shook his head. "No, but come on. She has tried to kill both of us. What makes you think that any other family member would be immune from that? It only makes sense."

"I think she buried the body—here in the cellar."

Luke looked at her and shook his head again. "What is it with her and cellars? Want a shovel?"

Ava was startled again. Luke was right that he knew the correct things to do, but he didn't always do them. It was past due to find out what had happened to their father, and he was happy to help out. However, Ava worried that Luke would tell their mother if she asked. She realised that it was too late now. They'd already had this talk.

"I think that the shovels are downstairs. Come on." Luke led the way, though Ava easily remembered where the door to the cellar was. Luke led the way downstairs, and she followed, worrying that Luke would do something to her.

The room was smaller than she remembered it. At least they would not be at it for hours like they had at her grandfather's house.

The floor was slightly damp, but the dirt had been packed so tight that she was unsure if they could dig down into the surface to release its secrets.

Luke took the shovel to the dirt against the far wall, but it barely cut through the dirt. "This is not going to be easy," he said. "Are you sure he's here?"

Ava shook her head. "Not at all. I'm just looking forward to the place where he might be buried. You need a big space to put an adult body."

"And it's heavy, too. I think this is probably not the place. You'd have to get the body down the stairs—and you'd have to do it without anyone seeing you. That's a big ask."

Ava thought again. The pub would always be busy, and this house would always have a family living in it. Even now, there were too many people coming and going to be considered secluded.

That left her grandfather's house with the fenced-in back

garden and the plants to make the garden less visible. The body could lay there for a day or two if need be. Only her grandfather would be out there, and after all she'd seen, Ava could easily believe that her mother and grandfather were in the crime together.

Ava had thought they'd searched every inch of the cellar, but in fact, she and George had been sidelined by the photos and the realisation that Vicki was not their aunt. They needed to do a more thorough investigation of the dirt—and the multitude of boxes that hid what had been buried beneath.

"Are you about done with me?" Luke asked, bringing her back to reality.

"Yeah, I was just thinking about Dad and a few of the good memories."

"Funny, I recall all the horrible things that happened to me, but I don't remember Dad much at all. I wish it were the other way around."

Ava nodded. Maybe her dad had saved her from behaving like Luke.

They went up the stairs, and Ava hugged Luke before heading back to the flat.

Chapter 29

Ava knew she would have to talk to her mother sooner rather than later. The time had come to head back to London and her job. She needed to remove herself from York and all the bad memories. Her flashbacks had become even worse as the weeks progressed, an issue she'd never had before this visit.

She wasn't sure what that meant for George and their relationship. That would be a difficult conversation and possibly a goodbye she didn't want. Yet she knew that York was not a good place for her, so she would have to be strong.

Ava decided that she would go back to her grandfather's cellar one more time and complete the search for her father's corpse. Of the three possible burial grounds, only one remained less than thoroughly investigated.

She took the shovel from the garage and headed downstairs.

The cellar looked far larger than it had when George was here with her. Then they had worked together. Now, she had to do the work by herself. Ava wasn't sure if she could move the boxes without assistance. They were packed with memories and photos of the family.

She'd only worked for about forty-five minutes downstairs when she heard voices in the house. At first, she hoped it was Luke coming to help her with the search, but she soon heard that the voices were female, two of them.

The pair had to be her mother and Vicki. Part of Ava wanted to throw her new knowledge in Vicki's face, but she decided that it would be futile. That woman was ruthless; any points she scored off her aunt would be paid back ten times. She had no compunction about what she did or who she did it to.

The voices were laughing now, and Ava was shocked by the fact that these women were enjoying themselves so soon after their father's loss, even if he had been a heartless abuser.

While she didn't want to talk to them, Ava did want to record their discussion. Maybe she could get enough information to show that Donna had destroyed the original will and planned to steal the house.

She put her phone on one of the top steps and pressed the record button. Ava went back to work, looking for a place where her father might be buried. She dug into the soft dirt, probing around for the remains. However, she found nothing.

The words ceased from upstairs, and Ava set down the shovel and headed for the stairs. The second stair creaked loudly, and Ava cursed the age of the house. She didn't want to alert anyone that she was there.

She took the phone and began to play it. Donna and Vicki were discussing the estate and the money that came with it.

"I've spent a good deal of money already on the house," Donna confessed. Ava recognised the tone of her voice, the faux apology that she'd heard so many times. The insincerity practically dripped from the phone.

Vicki laughed. "There are always ways to get more money. We had two fathers who showed us how to do it."

Ava was aghast. Vicki knew that her grandfather was not her father—that she'd been pawned off to an abuser who likely took advantage of her for years. What kind of "friend" would have done that to sate his friend's tastes?

The door to the cellar opened, and Ava knew she was trapped there. She put her phone in her pocket and picked up the shovel, thinking she might need to fend for herself here.

"Well, well," Donna said, walking down the stairs towards her daughter as Vicki followed behind. "Look what we have here. I thought I'd seen the last of you."

Vicki cackled. "And busy doing work on the house. How thoughtful."

Donna paused and then looked from one woman to the other. "She's down here looking for her father's grave. She thinks I killed him and stuffed his body down here." She laughed until she was crying. "That's too rich. There is something wrong with your head, don't forget, you are going around the twist, but don't take our word for it. Get yourself to the doctor. They will lock you up in a mental home where you belong. With all the other nutcases." Donna let out a laugh.

Vicki looked at Ava with those hateful eyes. "She certainly never learned any respect for you."

"Why would I respect you after what you've done?" Ava could feel her anger boil as she gripped the handle of the shovel.

"I guess Luke was right. All of this is coming back to her." Vicki's grin made her look as though she was pleased that Ava was recalling the abuse.

"I remember enough," Ava said, keeping an eye on both of them. She was dangerous to the women now, and they had shown that they were willing to kill anyone who got in their way.

"But not where the body is hidden?" Donna said. "You really think I killed that man and buried him in the garden or some other ridiculous place? Do you know so little about me?"

Ava could hear the woman start to use the pitiful, put-upon voice that she'd heard so many times as a child. Little had she known for years that it was all a ruse. The woman had been selling her out.

"Apparently, I don't. You sold your children to a group of

abusers who met in the Queen's Head pub. Did you participate?" Ava asked, not sure she wanted to answer.

Vicki laughed. "There are so many questions you could ask, and this is what you want to know? That's it?" Vicki moved closer to Ava. Even though she tried to look non-threatening, Ava was on the alert.

"We didn't touch you," Donna said with a look of disgust on her face. Ava was confused, thinking that the women seemed to be concerned with how they were perceived, even though Ava had evidence that they had participated in an abuse circle. She couldn't understand why they drew that line.

"Luke was another story. Such a young and very handsome child," Vicki said.

Ava felt sick to her stomach. Her mother and Vicki had participated in the abuse ring, not only running part of the business but abusing the children as well. She knew that she had to escape now—not later. These women would not want her to leave with all this knowledge. Police rules or not, this was an explosive amount of information.

"And the Robinson twins, too," added Donna.

"And how you're going to use the money you inherited," Ava said, not wanting to clue the two women in that she knew about the will. "You want to start it all again."

Donna smiled. "It made your grandfather millions. And then when he shut it down, he still asked for a small contribution from each member."

"Blackmail? He asked them for money in exchange for information."

"That's a harsh way to look at it. He was an entrepreneur, and Vicki and I plan to continue the legacy."

"And you want to buy the pub and start the abuse again. That's your big plan for the money."

"It's ideal," Vicki said. "With all your snooping, and yes,

we've heard all about it, you missed the security system that was installed. Cameras watching the outside and the bar, so we'd know if anyone had come in. The alarm system if someone played with the door. All the things you needed to make sure that no one interrupted the fun and games." She seemed almost proud of herself as she spoke.

Ava had no comment to make. Vicki was right about that. She had not seen those things at the pub.

"It makes sense to restart from there. Then we could continue without interruption."

Ava knew the best way to leave here in one piece was to split the women. Then, she would have two opponents, but they would not be working together. She could even get them to fight against each other instead.

"I might have missed that, but you missed one thing. When Donna destroyed the will—the one that your birth father signed, by the way—it cut you out of the will. The money and the house go to the next of kin. You're not a blood relative, so you get nothing, Vicki. Donna gets it all. You did all this work and won't inherit a thing." Ava hoped for some surprise and to fall out of the thieves. "Are you wondering why you haven't had to sign any papers? Donna signed them all, every last one, so you didn't know what was going on or how fast the estate was being processed through the probate courts. Usually, it takes years without a will."

"He'll be dead soon, and then that money will be mine—as the next of kin, as you say," Vicki said.

"You might want to check the books. He's not near as rich as my grandfather," Ava said. "You might get something, but that's it. The bulk of the abuse money will go to Donna. Then she can buy the pub and run things, and you'll have nothing."

Ava finished and watched the two women. Vicki tried to look complacent, but Ava could see the uncertainty as she frequently looked at Donna to reassure herself.

"What of it, Donna? Are you willing to sign over half the estate to Vicki right here and now? I'll gladly witness the document. It wouldn't take more than a minute to sign, and then we could all be happy."

Donna didn't appear to be happy. She looked from her daughter to her sister and then back again. She didn't speak, and Ava knew she was trying to think of a way to control Vicki without giving her a penny.

Donna began pacing the cellar as she pondered, with Vicki watching her every move. Donna had yet to talk about her plans with the fortune.

The silence gave Ava her opening. Still carrying the shovel, she moved slowly towards the stairs. She stumbled over a lump on the floor and looked down. The fingers of a decayed body were part of the way through the floor where she'd been digging earlier.

Donna and Vicki stopped and looked over, too. In that second, they became a pair against the outsiders again, not two women fighting over a fortune.

"Well, on the bright side, you'll have the chance to be buried with your father," Donna said, pulling a gun from her pocket.

Ava had to think fast, and she decided to blackmail these two and turn the situation around. "I wouldn't if I were you," she said. She pulled out the phone, which was awkward, given that she carried the shovel in her other hand. She pressed the button, and the audio began to play. Donna and Vicki were planning to recruit some children for their new "venture."

"I wouldn't do anything to harm me because I've informed several people—including a few in London—that if anything happens to me to play this recording." Ava pressed a few buttons and sent the audio to George. She didn't care if she lied at this point. Her mother, who had tried to poison her, now had a gun on her.

"We can delete it from her phone," Vicki said. "Then it will appear to be a hoax."

Donna snorted. "It's not that easy. The police could find it in a snap on her phone and see what she sent to others. You can't lie about the digital world. It's there forever."

Ava felt a small amount of relief. Perhaps one of them had a certain amount of sense regarding technology.

"I'm going to walk out of here, and you won't stop me."

Donna stared at her daughter with malevolence in her eyes. "And you're not going to stop me either."

She lifted the gun, aimed, and fired a shot that hit the stairs inches from Ava's head. Ava screamed while the two women laughed. "You'll say nothing about this. You've already gone to the police once with your crazy stories. Do you think they'll believe you now?"

Ava took a few steps toward the door. The stairs squeaked again, and Ava winced. She could feel the threat of her mother. Another shot was fired, and Ava began to hurry up the stairs regardless of the noise and consequences. Her mother wanted her dead.

Donna and Vicki had said nothing, which scared her even more. They were probably already planning what the next step would be. Ava was determined that she would also plan to save the children of York from these two women.

She opened the door and then pushed it shut, locking it behind her. It wouldn't hold them for long, but enough time for her to get away.

Chapter 30

Ava was still crying when George came home. She had begun as soon as she had returned to the flat, and now she felt like she couldn't stop. Her world, as bad as it was, had become worse.

Thinking about the past week, she'd realised that she'd been abused by three family members, though her mother and Vicki had denied it. They were so graphic about Luke that their words were worth nothing. She'd learned that they'd made a fortune from an abuse ring that included many people in York. Donna had taken the will and destroyed it. She had stolen the estate from her children, and now her mother, as if she had any right to that title, had killed her father and poisoned and shot at Ava.

And the police did nothing to stop any of it. Donna was going to walk away from the entire disgusting situation and live her life with other people's money.

George finally got Ava to stop crying, though it took nearly an entire box of tissues.

"Sometimes it's painful, but you have to look at what you've learned," George said, stroking her hand.

"It's painful. I knew my home life was bad, but it's like opening the door and realising that your mother is not just a bad mother. She is a criminal and the abuser of children — including her own. How sick can that be?" Ava gasped air like she was going to cry again, but she stopped herself before it started.

"I'll get you a cup of tea, and we can talk more," George

said. "Then we can make a plan."

Ava thought she might be sick, but she leaned far into the pillows on the sofa and tried to push everything out of her mind. She realised how unhealthy that was and how it had put her in this position. George was right. She needed to confront what had happened and put herself back together.

He brought the steaming liquid and a big smile. "When you get to London, you'll need to talk to a therapist, not one who is a friend, and they can help you work through his."

"I'm happy to help, but I can't be your therapist," George said. His face looked concerned as he spoke.

"You've been so helpful," Ava began, but George cut her off.

"I have helped, but I can't be the therapist of someone I care about. That's unethical, and I wouldn't want that to get in the way..." He trailed off without finishing the sentence.

"The way of what?" Ava asked, though she was sure she had the answer.

"Of us dating," he finished. "A therapist can't date or get serious with a client."

"That's going to be hard to do," Ava said. "I'll be in London, and you'll be here in York. I'm not sure how long-distance works."

"There are millions of people in need of mental health in London," George said. "I'm sure I could find some clients there—just not you."

She laughed. "There are one or two—I've met them."

"I think when you get started, you'll find out that Donna did two levels of abuse to you. The big stuff is obvious. She gave you to men who wanted to abuse you. She stole from you. She tried to harm you. However, there are several things she did that were less noticeable but messed with your self-esteem. Those will have a big impact when you start recognising them and working your way past them."

"Like what?" Ava asked. She thought almost every one of the things Donna did was horrible. She had never tried to scale them between better and worse.

"The poison. It wasn't made to kill you, or so the doctor said. I think that Donna just miscalculated the dosage. She hadn't had a chance to do that in a decade or so. She guessed and guessed wrong. She wanted to keep you weak and dependent on her. The holes in your pocket that you mentioned to me once in passing. You thought they were mice, but it was Donna again. She made it so you'd lose things, and things would fall out of your pockets. It would make you appear forgetful and unorganised. Again, you'd need to rely on Donna to mend the pockets so you wouldn't lose things."

"But..." Ava said. "Why did she want me reliant on her?" George seemed to know this pattern, and it somehow calmed Ava to learn that many other people had similar situations. They'd come out of it, much as she had. She was not alone. She was not a less-than-adequate person. Her job had helped establish her own pride in herself. This would add to it, allowing her to be more confident in her sales work.

"For starters, to do the big crimes against you. She could make you want to please her since she was taking care of you. Then, you wouldn't make a terrible fuss when she took you to the pub's cellar. Look at how Luke is. He had another decade of Donna's abuse, and he thinks selling himself for cash is an appropriate way of living. And he refuses to deal with Donna's abuse. He praises her. I wonder what would happen to him if the police ever did arrest Donna. He'd be devastated."

She thought about that. Luke would not know how to function in a world where his mother t didn't care for him. He'd be in his mid-thirties and never have been on his own. What a fate.

Ava looked at him, and for the first time in ages, she felt good about herself. She was going to get away from York—and Luke would be coming with her. She had a relationship with someone who knew her flaws and past and still cared about her.

Ava jumped when the phone rang. She was sure that Donna had called to threaten her into staying silent. She wasn't sure what she wanted to do. Her options were limited since the police had rejected her pleas for help. So, she would either need to come up with tangible evidence or walk away.

George made a motion, and Ava nodded. He picked up her mobile and identified himself. As soon as he did, he put the phone on speaker so they both could hear.

A raspy voice said, "I need to talk to Ava Hedges."

There was a long pause, and then a softer voice spoke. "Hello, my name is Father Greene. I'm at the hospital with Alfred Cook. According to the doctors, he's not likely to make it through the night. However, he made a confession to me. He asked me to write it down and then give it to you. Would it be possible for you to come here?"

Ava's eyes widened. She had never expected that the sarcastic abuser who had denied everything had a change of heart.

"We'll be right there," Ava replied, and George clicked off the phone.

George had driven, and she was glad about it. Several times during the ride, her hands shook. She couldn't believe what she'd heard, and she'd come so close so many times before that she wouldn't believe the story until she had the paper in her hands. Ava feared they would be too late, and the confession would be lost.

Ava recalled the path from her last unsuccessful visit and guided George to the man's room. This time, Alfred Cook was not alone. Ava saw a man with a collar, who had to be Father Greene and a nurse. Fearing that time was running short, Ava moved quickly into the room.

Alfred was the first to speak—a voice that was hard to hear between the coughs punctuating his sentences every few seconds. "I'm glad you came. The father here told me I needed to apologise and make amends before I go. He seems to feel that I would be forgiven. I'm not too sure about that. I did some awful things." Cook started another coughing bout that lasted several minutes. "Anyway, I confessed to the father. With my permission, he wrote up what I'd said to him. The paper is right here." He pointed to a single sheet of paper that lay on the table that crossed his bed. "If you want it. I trust that you'll do the right thing with it."

Alfred coughed again, and the priest spoke. "I signed my name at the top and bottom of the page," he said. "I hope that's enough."

Ava knew what was needed from her real estate career. "Get a notary, please," she asked with a tinge of urgency.

The nurse nodded. "There's one in the main office." She picked up the phone and punched in a few numbers. Ava wondered if they got strange requests like this often. The nurse didn't seem upset by the events, and the notary quickly said she was on her way.

The woman arrived in a few minutes. Alfred Cook signed the paper, and she stamped it and signed it as well. The document looked as formal as a real estate document. However, Ava wasn't done. She took the names and phone numbers of the priest, the nurse, and the notary as well. She wanted to have as many witnesses as possible, along with their contact information.

After that, the nurse agreed to make twenty copies of the document. She came back with a sheaf of papers bound with a binder clip. Ava finally felt that she could relax and breathe now.

"What are you doing with all those papers?" Cook asked. His voice was softer now, and Ava could detect a wheeze in his chest. She wondered if she should let Vicki know. Would there be a reason to reunite them after all this time?

"I'm not sure yet, but I don't trust Donna if she knows they exist. I'll probably send one to my address in London. Another to a friend, and then I'll start delivering them to the police. Maybe this will get their attention."

The man nodded, not even trying to talk now.

"Do you want me to call Vicki?" Ava asked finally.

"You got that far, did ya?" the man asked. "You did good. Nah, I'm not going to try to mend that fence."

"I found that out, and I learned a great deal more." Ava looked out the window, trying to think of what to tell him next.

Cook pulled a paper from under the mattress. "This is for you too," he said, pushing it toward Ava.

Ava read the first few paragraphs and stopped. Cook was leaving his entire estate to Ava. She was repulsed thinking that she and Luke—along with countless others—had paid for that money as part of the victims of the abuse ring. "I don't think I can take it," she said.

"I heard Vicki and your mum were trying to start things back up. I don't want the money to get into their hands. I know now that what I did was wrong, and I don't want to perpetuate that crime."

Ava nodded. She knew of many charity organisations that would accept a donation of this size. It could be used in so many good ways, and anything would be better than letting those two women have it.

The man seemed to be fading. His eyes flickered, and his breath grew slower. She and George left the hospital without talking.

Chapter 31

Ava looked through the peephole of the flat door and braced herself. Donna stood on the other side of the entrance.

"Love, let me in. It's been too long since we've seen each other."

Ava recognised the technique. Her mother would pretend that nothing had happened—in this case, shooting at her with a gun—and that they were the best of friends, a close-knit family who visited each other routinely.

George looked at Ava and shrugged. He was right. The decision had to be hers, and no one else. She took a deep breath, nodded to George, and opened the door.

Donna walked into the flat and turned to give Ava a big hug. Part of Ava worried that she had a knife that would slide into her back at any second. However, Donna made no movements to threaten her.

She looked at George, who returned the smile. Her eyes squinted as Ava's beau monitored her. "What have you been up to? I haven't seen you in ages."

"Not since you tried to shoot me," Ava said, giving the same mock smile back to her mother. "It makes one less likely to come around."

"Oh, Ava, you're exaggerating again. The gun went off by accident. Vicki found it on the shelves and didn't bother to check the safety. I've told her a hundred times to be more careful. You should know that. I don't see why that should scare you away." Donna, without invitation, walked into the flat. She did a quick survey of the living room and then checked out the bedroom.

Donna looked like she was going to say something, but she chose not to. Ava was relieved. This was no time to talk to her mother about the facts of life. Ava was far past that age.

"Could I get a drink of water?" Donna asked. "I could die of thirst, waiting for an invitation."

Ava wished that were true, but she went into the kitchen, grabbed three glasses, and filled them with water from the fridge door.

She brought them out to the living room, where Donna seemed to be asking George a litany of questions. "Well, I'm not sure. You'd really have to ask Ava," George replied for the third time in a row.

"Ask me what?" Ava asked as she set a glass in front of Donna and two in front of George and her own seat.

"I just wanted to know if you had made any permanent plans for the two of you?" Donna asked the question like it was commonplace.

"It's only been a few weeks so far, but we're continuing to see each other."

Donna started to ask something else and reached for the glass. Her hand hit the glass, which then went splashing onto the floor.

Ava picked up the glass and went to refill it. George went to the kitchen to get a rag to wipe up the mess. "What do you think of this?" Ava asked him.

"She might be wanting to start over. She could feel like she's losing her control over you and wants to reassert herself. It's hard to say. I don't know her."

When they came back out with the rag and a new glass of water, Donna had that look on her face. The same one she'd had while making Ava and Luke dinner, the same look when she let off the gun in the cellar. Donna was a dangerous woman and right now, she was at the most lethal moment.

Ava had to stop for a second, not putting the water glass on the coffee table. What had Donna done? Where was the danger?

Her first thought was poison, the most common of Donna's attacks. Then she realised they were out of the room when Donna was here with the two glasses — alone and doing who knew what.

Ava plastered on the smile again and walked to the table. "I was concerned that the glass might be dirty. Here, why don't you drink this one," Ava said putting the glass on the table and offering her Ava's untouched glass of water.

Donna took the glass and drank the entire glass in one gulp. Her mother had no fear about this glass. That meant — she paused as she realised that Donna must have tainted George's glass with poison.

She took George's glass and handed it to Donna. "You must be dreadfully thirsty. Have this one, too." She pushed the glass close to Donna's face, waiting for her to refuse the glass.

Donna smacked the glass which sent it flying across the room. It hit the wall and shattered. The poisoned water ran down the wall in a dangerous stream.

"You were going to poison George, just like you poisoned me, just like you poisoned Luke. You have to be in charge. You have to have control. What is the matter with you?"

"There's nothing wrong with me, dear. I don't know what you're talking about. You're always imagining that I'm doing things to you. It's a good thing that you have a therapist living here. Maybe he can help you with your issues. You've had them since you were a child, and they've never gotten any better. I do wish you all the best in becoming sane. All of us would appreciate it. You always come out smelling of roses, don't you?" With that, Donna turned and left the flat.

"Wow, that was worse than I even thought. She pulled out all the stops on that. You need therapy—to get over Donna Hedges. That's for sure. The rest of it was gaslighting. I feel for you. That couldn't have been easy as a child."

Ava nodded and looked at the mess again. The chaos was all part of what she'd experienced and what she would now need to overcome.

"How do you clean up poison?" George asked. He laughed as he asked.

Ava joined in with the stress and anger release.

When the laughter subsided, George looked at her. "You know we can't let this go. She tried to poison you, overdose Luke, and now tried to poison me. She's a menace to all of York at this rate."

"But—," Ava started.

"If you're worried about the police, there are two of us now. Donna overplayed her hand this time. It's one thing to find poison in a cup where people come and go as your mother did with you, but there were only three of us in the flat. If you didn't do it and I didn't do it, then it had to be Donna. Then you can add to your case, and it's a likely conviction. She should be very worried."

Ava recalled the times when her mother had been caught before. "She's dangerous when she's cornered."

"More dangerous than trying to kill both of us?" George asked. "Don't worry. Now there's someone who believes in you and knows what Donna is like."

George looked at her. "There's only one way to end this, and that's to confront her with all her crimes and abuses. It will let her know where you stand, and it will give you some closure."

"I've seen her at her worst," Ava said. She looked at the paperwork on the table. "Do you mind if we stop at the post office on the way to my mother's house? I have something I really need to send off."

After stopping at the post office, they pulled up in front of Donna's home. Ava felt odd parking in a spot visible from the house. She had grown used to parking at a distance, so her mother wasn't aware of her presence. Now it was the other way around, perhaps Donna did not want them to know she was there.

The house was still when they walked into the kitchen. Ava had no desire to call out for her mother. The upcoming confrontation would be difficult, and she wasn't looking forward to it.

There was no sign of Luke either.

"She might be hiding out at my grandfather's house now. After all, she thinks it's hers."

"Thinks?" George asked.

"I mailed off the will to a solicitor in London. I am hoping he can file for this probate, and I can get the money due to me."

George raised an eyebrow at her. "I hadn't expected that, but good on you. You're standing up for what is right and what is yours. Did you tell Luke?"

Ava shook her head. "I knew that if I told him, he would tell Donna, and she might try to stop the probate—or stop me. This is better. Let the law handle it."

"Do you want to look around?" George asked. "She could be hiding."

Ava laughed, which resounded through the house. "She's never run from a fight before. I can't imagine that she'll hide from this one."

They walked into the living room, but nothing looked out of place. Ava did notice that the photos and a few pieces of memorabilia had gone missing.

"Could we go upstairs?" Ava asked. "I just had an idea."

Ava led the way to the first floor, and they walked down the hallway. She knocked and opened Luke's door. There was no answer. She silently opened the door and looked in. Nothing had changed. The room looked identical to the way it had when Ava had found Luke on the bed.

She closed the door and went to her old room. She opened the door and gasped. The furniture was overturned, the bed was slashed, and her clothes had been destroyed by bleach and other destructive products.

George looked in after her. "Not much to take back to London, eh?"

Ava looked into his eyes. "This is not good. We're in for a battle."

George nodded, and they headed to Donna's room.

Ava didn't bother to knock. She knew no one was there. Donna was not the type to fume. She was the sort to act. She'd be gone by now, licking her wounds and planning her next steps. From the look of Ava's room, those steps would be violent and sudden.

The room was nearly empty. The large furniture was still in place, but all signs of personal touches had vanished. Ava could see no clothes in the wardrobe. The linens had disappeared. Ava ran a quick inventory through the dresser and found nothing.

"She's gone," Ava said.

"Where do you think she'd be?" George asked.

"Grandfather's house. She can stay there until things calm down." Ava wondered how long that would be—until Ava left York. Or would it take longer for the chaos to subside?

"Then I think it's about time we had a family discussion and a few more for good measure. Would you text Vicki and Luke?"

Ava sent both of them a nearly identical message, asking

them to attend a meeting at the other house. In the background, she could hear George asking the police to attend as well.

When they went back downstairs, the blue ceramic cup on the table took on a new meaning to Ava. "Do you think that Donna was using this cup to poison me? Is that what she's trying to tell me?"

George took a napkin and picked up the cup. "I think it's far more sinister than that." He pointed to the white coating on the inside of the glass. "I think this might be what made you sick before."

"She smeared the inside of the glass, so I was the only one to use it and the only one to get sick. Then it made it look like a nervous illness rather than a way to make just one person sick. No wonder she pulled out that crappy-looking cup when I came home. I always hated that cup—now I know why. Luke had one of those cups as well. I would be willing to bet that she used it on him, too."

"Take it with you. We might need that for the police," George said. They located a plastic bag and carried it out with them.

This was about to get interesting, Ava thought as she climbed into the car.

Chapter 32

When they pulled up in front of Arthur Farley's home, Ava could see signs of life. A lamp was on in the upstairs floor, something new to the house. It had not shown any signs of occupancy since Ava had arrived in York.

Vicki came storming down the path and stopped at the car. "What is this all about? Why are you insisting on this meeting?" Ava first noticed the color of her eyes, which were dark brown rather than green. She wondered if Vicki had ever determined her heritage before now. Had she recognised being the only one with dark eyes? She had stood out even then.

Luke had followed her, but he didn't say a word.

"You'll see. Things need to change, and it's long overdue."

Vicki snorted. "You mean, you need to go back to London and forget all this. That's what you're best at. I'm glad to see that you brought a therapist. You need one."

"You'll see, Miss Cook," Ava said, referring to the woman by her birth name. Ava wondered again if Vicki's mind had done the same thing, forgetting all the evil from her past—and cleaning her memory of the horrible past.

"How dare you? Is this meeting going to be one long accusation? If it is, I'll leave now."

Ava made her face as neutral as possible. "I wouldn't do that. You will want to hear the evidence against you regarding the criminal accusations against her."

With the mention of crime, Vicki grew silent.

Ava pointed to the door. "Let's go in. We need to talk."

Luke and Vicki barged ahead of them and opened the door

without knocking. Ava and George followed behind them. Ava took the time to look for bulges that might indicate another weapon, but she saw nothing.

Just inside was Donna, standing there and oozing hate like one of the Greek Furies.

"What are you doing here? Didn't you get enough of me earlier?" Donna said. She stood still, not sure what was happening here. "Are you going to close the door or cost me a fortune in utilities?"

George waited for a few seconds until two men in police uniforms and a man in a suit and tie entered the room. Ava assumed he was the man in charge.

"Now we can get started," George said. They had talked on the way over, and once everyone was there, the party would belong to Ava.

"Let's start at the beginning. I came here to mourn for my grandfather. I won't be doing that anymore. Shortly after his funeral, I took my brother to the hospital, thinking that he had attempted suicide. I learned from my brother that he had been abused by him. It seemingly led to Luke's suicide attempt. However, I later learned that my mother, Donna, had been behind that incident. She wanted Luke to look unstable, so anything he might say would be taken lightly."

Luke started to sputter a denial, but Ava stopped him.

"The pills used had expired and were not as potent as medicine that is still viable. Therefore, the question became whether Donna had wanted him dead or just to scare or threaten him. While Luke was recovering, he shared that my grandfather and others had abused him as a child. He indicated that I had been abused as well."

"Shortly after, I began to have painful flashbacks that indicated I'd been abused as well. Luke and I compared experiences, and we both recalled the cellar of a pub. I later learned that the pub was called the Queen's Head and later renamed the Prince Gentleman's Pub. The Queen's Head had been owned by two men, my grandfather and a man named Alfred Cook. They ran an abuse ring from which they made a great deal of money."

Vicki spoke up. "That's all hearsay and your imagination. Nothing like that happened."

Ava shot back. "This woman is the daughter of Alfred Cook. I am not sure why she was raised by my grandfather, but I suspect that it was for illegal reasons. Her birth father is on his deathbed, and he told me what happened."

"That shows you what you know. He died last night," Donna said with a certain amount of glee in her voice. "You have no witness to testify to that. It's all your word against mine."

Ava nodded. "He was on his deathbed, so he wrote down all the things that had happened, including the building, the abuse, and the names of some of the children. He had it notarized, and there were two other witnesses at the event. One of them is a priest."

George handed a copy of the letter to the plain-clothed policeman, who took it and read the contents. His expression was much more severe when he looked at Donna and Vicki again. "This looks to be authentic. Deathbed confessions are still allowed in a court of law."

"While I began digging up some of this information, I was also poisoned," Ava said, continuing with the narrative. "The doctor said that I had ingested rat poison, which is available at my mother's home. The doctor said that there were indications that I had been poisoned several times over my stay at her house."

"You did it to yourself. We all ate the same things and drank the same drinks—we were just fine, Luke and I both."

"You got carried away. You left that blue ceramic cup on the kitchen table for me. Inside of the cup were dregs of some white material. It's being tested as we speak. I hope to have the results soon. That explains why you wanted us to use named cups long after we were adults."

George spoke. "The same for the drink you knocked out of my hand. We collected the shards of the glass and contents and sent them off. At the time, Ava, her mother, and I were the only three people in the room. That would mean that Donna was responsible for the attempted murder of at least three people. Given those attempts, we've retained a solicitor who is petitioning a judge right now to exhume Arthur Farley's body to see if he was poisoned as well."

"I did no such thing. I'm not a monster. You make me out to be a serial killer. I'm just a mother with two ill children." Donna's face had grown angry as the various crimes had been explained to the police. "Ava's always had issues, always had mental illness. You should know that. She's not to be believed. She was always getting sick. She had anxiety attacks. She threw up all the time as a child."

George shook his head. He turned to the policemen. "I've seen signs of psychosis, and I strongly suspect that she has Factitious disorder on another person, or most likely known to you as Munchausen syndrome by proxy. She has been injuring her children physically to get attention while also exposing them to abuse. I don't think it would be possible for the children to be gone for hours with their grandfather and not see signs of abuse."

"So far, we have three counts of attempted murder, a possible case of fratricide, sexual abuse, and organised sexual abuse. You got anything more?" the plainclothes policeman asked.

"Well, I think that they killed my grandfather to get his

estate so they could get the money to start up the sex abuse ring again. He'd been sick for years, and their child abuse ring had to stop because both men were ill. They wanted the money that belonged to my grandfather to restart their criminal scheme. I don't know what the charges would be for that—or how far they got with their arrangement—but that would be another charge."

"Do you want to say anything in your defense, Donna Hedges? I have a hunch I'll be reading you your rights shortly, but you can always tell us your side of the story."

"The house and money were mine," Donna started. "It all belonged to me. Just me."

Vicki looked at her "sister" and then at the police. "Would there be any sort of sentencing reduction if one of us were to confess and tell the police about the real mastermind of this scheme?"

"That could be arranged," the policeman said. "We do that kind of thing all the time."

"Damn it, Vicki, I meant us, I meant ours. You're going to give me away just because of a slip of the tongue? Think of what we're missing out."

Vicki shook her head. "I've been thinking about this since Ava mentioned it. You wanted it all for yourself and didn't care how you got it. Every last penny."

"Well, not all of it," Ava said. "I sent the original will to a solicitor friend of mine, and he's filing that document to probate. Luke and I will get the money we deserve."

The policeman cleared his throat. "Well, if half of these things are true, then your mother will have sacrificed her rights. She can't just kill people to get their money—and then keep that money. It will go to the next of kin. Who would that be?" he asked.

"My brother and I," Ava said, thinking of the outrage that

Donna would have had to have done all this cruelty and abuse—only to have it taken away.

"As long as you're not a participant in the murder of your grandfather, then you'll both be very wealthy people in the near future. Now, is there anything else, or are we done here?"

Ava cleared her throat. "I think there's one more thing. I believe the bones that are in the cellar are the skeleton of my father, who I thought abandoned us when I was a young girl."

Before the policeman could respond, Luke shouted out. "That's not true. None of this is true. I've stood here and listened to all these lies. Every last one of these lies, and they just keep going on. I'll never believe that my mother killed her husband, her father, and tried to kill both of us. She's not like that. She's a good person. Why don't you see that, Ava? You've always hated her and blamed her for everything that happened."

"McAllister, would you go downstairs and see if that's true? It would go a long way to see who is telling the truth if bones are in the cellar."

The entourage waited for a few minutes while the policeman excused himself. Ava felt the anxiety run through her. What if Donna had removed all the bones in the time between her discovery and now? Then she would look like the liar, and Donna would escape all the charges. Ava couldn't bear the thought of her mother's crimes going unpunished.

McAllister returned, his face pale and his eyes wide. "Something is down there for sure."

"What?" The detective asked.

McAllister swallowed. "It looks like a femur and probably a knee. We have to search the entire cellar. This is a crime scene. I want backup, and I want the whole house sealed off until we can do a proper investigation."

The plain-clothed detective looked at Ava again. "And you

say that it's your father down there, and your mother killed him."

Ava nodded. "Either because he found out about the abuse ring or because my mother wanted her father's growing estate all for herself. She went as far as to have him declared dead so that there would be no claim against the estate."

"You want her to hang, don't you? Nothing else will make you happy. You're worse than she is, and I never thought I'd say that. You were supposed to be on my side. What am I going to do now? What am I going to do?" Luke began to cry, and he turned and walked away. No one stopped him.

Ava cringed, but she had somewhat expected this. Luke always seemed to tell her about the abuses of her mother, and then he'd turn around and defend her again. She sighed. People really didn't ever change, and Ava felt certain that Luke had too many years of believing his mother's lies and her insistence that he rely on her. He couldn't take away that prop and admit the truth.

The truth that Ava could handle was that she and Luke could never forge a new and healthy relationship. It would always be flawed — if they could ever have one.

Donna began to kick and scream as the two uniformed policemen read her the rights and handcuffed her.

They walked her out the door, and as she left, Donna turned to face Ava. "You always come out smelling of roses, don't you?" Then she spat on Ava.

Chapter 33

Ava had agreed to meet George at Millenium Bridge. It was an odd place to start a date night, but she was curious enough to want to go. Her group session had ended late, and she was rushing to find a taxi to get her there on time.

The city buzzed by as the taxi driver gave her a quick tour of the tourist spots in London. She didn't bother to correct him that she was now a homeowner in the city. After completing the probate, she and Luke received the entire estate to share equally. A fortune that came to over ten million pounds was hers. Ava had some concerns about taking this money, given its source. Still, George had told her she could donate generously to charities while also enjoying it. After all, she, too, had been a victim of the child abuse ring.

Luke had not thanked Ava for her help in getting the matter resolved. He hadn't even acknowledged her. Ava forced him to sell their grandfather's house since he had no desire to live there more than she had. The money and funds from the house gave Ava enough not to work. Still, she'd chosen to stay in real estate, enjoying interacting with people and starting a new phase of her life. She'd picked a house for her—and one that perhaps George would live in. She'd even received a discount since she was one of the leading agents in the company.

She thought about George and wondered what was going on with him at the moment. He had moved to London shortly after Ava had returned to the city. His new office with a flood of clients kept him busy. They still made time for each other, even with their busy schedules. However, date night was usually on Saturdays, and this was a Wednesday evening. George had been secretive about the reasons for the meeting on the bridge, but he'd been adamant that she not be late.

Yet here she was, a few minutes late, with five minutes to the bridge. The taxi swerved in front of another car and pulled up the waiting George on the bridge.

Always the kind man, George helped her out of the taxi and tipped the driver—with a generous tip from the man's comments.

"So, what's so important on a Wednesday night?" Ava asked, watching the water flow peacefully under the bridge.

"A celebration. How was work?" he asked.

"I think I sold the flat in Chelsea," she said, feeling the pride well up in her. Six months ago, she could never have admitted that she had done the work and felt pride in a well-done job. Then, it would have been claiming luck or someone else helping her with the sale.

"And I'm guessing you ran late because of the group session?" George asked. "Helping someone else?"

She nodded. Ava didn't often talk about the group sessions, but she faithfully attended them two times a week. Over the past year, as she shared her story, Ava had also found ways to help others in the group. She would never have thought that her story would help others—or that so many others had similar stories. Each time she shared, it made it easier to come to grips with the horror of her childhood. The pain grew less, and her happiness grew abundantly. She lost her embarrassment and shame with that.

"Well, I heard good news today," George said. "The sentencing was completed today, and Donna will be spending the rest of her life in prison. She has no chance of returning to society and having contact with you. I thought you'd be happy to hear that."

"What about the rest?" Ava asked. Many people had been involved in the crime, and she hoped they all faced consequences.

"Vicki got a reduced sentence for ratting out Donna, but it's still twenty years. At her age, that might as well be a life sentence. And since you seem to be her only 'next of kin,' the judge also mandates that the money from the Cook estate be sent to you."

Ava smiled. "When do you have time to work when you are busy doing all these other things?"

"I just wanted to see this all taken care of. I want you to be able to move on without worries about these women and what they did. You're free now. Here's to happiness."

Ava pondered for a second. "Not happy, but relieved. I wish she had made better choices and lived a better life, but if she's not going to do that, then I'm relieved that she won't be able to abuse anyone else."

George held up a plastic envelope that he brought in a carrier bag. He moved it closer so Ava could see the dreaded blue ceramic cup. "I thought we might do something to celebrate the end of that era," George said.

Ava looked at it again. She could still see the white streaks of poison on the sides of the cup. The cup reminded her of the past and a far worse time. It was hard to believe she'd ever heard her mother's lies. Ava was not a hypochondriac, and she wasn't mentally ill. That had just been her mother's projection on her daughter rather than herself.

"What shall we do with it?" Ava asked.

"I thought perhaps we could permanently get rid of it. To celebrate the end of one life and the start of another."

Ava liked the sound of that. She wanted to move ahead and not think of her past life. That life was gone and would never come back. She would see to that. There would be problems and obstacles in her life, but the tears of the abuse and the betrayal of her family were behind her. She could not change the past. She would not allow the past to hold her back. She would accept it and move on.

George put the plastic envelope on the ground. Ava jumped up and landed both feet on the cup. It smashed into dozens of little pieces. She was glad that the envelope had not split. She was done picking up after others.

George then pulled out a bottle of champagne and two flutes for them. He popped the cork, looking around for any policemen to tell them to put the alcohol away. He poured the bubbly into the glasses and waited until some fizz had gone down. "To us," George said.

"To the future," Ava replied.

They clinked their glasses, and each took a sip. Ava knew that George had paid good money for the champagne; it was far better than what they served at the real estate office. So much had changed, and so much looked rosy for the future. Ava laughed before she took another sip.

When they were finished, George put the flutes and champagne back in the carrier bag. "More for when we get home," he said with a smile.

He picked up the envelope and threw it into the bin. When George returned, she gave him a long kiss, not embarrassed to show affection to someone who cared for her. When the kiss ended, she took his hand, and they walked away from the cup and the past.

END

Afterword

They say you can't pick your family, but my spiritual journey has taught me that you do. Our life is all about experience, learning, and growing, only achieved by giving out different roles to play - the good, bad, and ugly. Once I accepted this, I could forgive, let go, and live a more joyful and peaceful life.

The greater the hardship, the greater the potential for growth along the paths of strength and determination. I just had to change my perspective.

The most magnificent beings that ever lived, endured the toughest of times—you know who you are. I salute you.

Printed in Great Britain
by Amazon